Elketh handed her the arrow. Their fingers brushed against each other as Ruga took it. "I used to pick up women like this," Elketh said.

"What?"

"It was a good excuse for a lot of touching," she said, and then shrugged like it meant nothing. "I have to confess that while I'm good at archery, I'm not a very good teacher."

Ruga set the arrow into place with the knowledge she had from watching Elketh's form. She kept her shoulder low instead of letting it ride up, and then raised her other elbow so it was aligned with her arm nearest Elketh and the arrow. Elketh might not be a good teacher, but Ruga was a quick learner. "Were you flirting with me?" Ruga asked finally, the bow taut.

HUMAN TERRITORY
ELVEN ISLANDS
Northgate
Vakker
Ceridwen
OLWEN
LYNBY
Westgate
TORDEN
ANWEN
BRANWEN
Ravn
Ulfur's Base
ORC COUNTRY
Sydlig Forest
AEGIR OCEAN
DWYRAIN OCEAN
SYDLIG
TORDEN
AND SURROUNDING ENVIRONS

ALSO BY LILA GWYNN

OLYMPIA THE BOUNTY HUNTER

Kissed the Mark

Falling for the Fugitive

Undead at Large

THE SAPPHIC ORCS OF TORDEN

The Orc and Her Bride

The Orc and Her Spy

The Orc and Her Captive

STANDALONE

The Yuletide Fairy's Curse

SHORT FICTION

"The Scavenger of the Skies" (Indie Bites, Vol. 7)

"A Curse Is on Her If She Stay" (Indie Bites, Vol. 9)

"Here Be Salt and Dragons" (Indie Bites, Vol. 10)

"Blooming in Brimstone" (She Was Monstress, Vol. 1)

"The Wedding Heist of Ellen o' the Dale" (Indie Bites, Vol. 18)

THE ORC —AND— HER BRIDE

BOOK ONE OF THE SAPPHIC ORCS OF TORDEN

LILA GWYNN

Eldest of Three

The Orc and Her Bride

Cover & map design by Sarah Waites at The Illustrated Page Book Design
https://theillustratedpage.net/design/

Published by Eldest of Three
https://lilagwynn.com

ISBN-13 (eBook): 979-8-9853385-5-3
ISBN-13 (Paperback): 979-8-9853385-6-0

For information about content warnings, spice level, and happily ever afters, please visit: https://lilagwynn.com/books/sapphic-orcs-of-torden

For prickly women who deserve love too

CHAPTER ONE

The storm was a bad omen.

Elketh didn't believe in such superstitions. It was her last day of freedom, and not even bad omens could interfere with her plans. By sundown, Elketh's father would call her into his study and inform her whom he had selected for her to marry. At the end of the fifty-day engagement period to become acquainted with her betrothed, her father would finally retire, and Elketh would become elf queen of Branwen, something she had anticipated since she was just a seventy-year-old girl.

Elketh Ceridwen used up her last day the way she would spend every day of her life, if she could—calling on old lovers to share one last roll in the hay (or the stable, or their mother's bed, or at the glen behind the orchard). Her father was lenient about just one thing: Elketh had a strong preference for women, so he promised that her future spouse would be one. There were other things he was not so lenient about, namely that she would have to be loyal to her bride, and she wasn't permitted to be involved in the choosing. Elketh had her eye on one of the Olwen daughters, a buff elf named Rhiannon whom Elketh often admired swinging a sword around whenever the Ceridwens had to conduct their diplomatic visits to the other Elven Islands. She dropped hints about this whenever she could, inquiring after Rhiannon in front of the king and discussing her crush with her brother when she knew her father was listening.

If there was one thing Elketh had inherited from her father, though, it was his stubbornness, and his unwillingness to do anything he was told.

Truthfully, Elketh was excited to meet her new life partner. There was something enticing about the excuse it gave her to break off prior attachments. Not to mention the excuse it gave her to make one last request for an amorous encounter, to which hardly any of them had said no. More than that, she anticipated inheriting the throne and the island it ruled over. She already had a list of changes she was going to make—starting with the drab gray clothing the servants wore. Elketh thought her father a dusty old fool who didn't like things to be different than they were.

After her fourth amorous encounter of the day, when Elketh struggled to stand after a particularly rough go of it, she steadied herself against a stable's doorframe and caught her breath as the horses snorted around her. Fipple—or whatever her name was; Elketh could never—was already gone, buckling her trousers as she walked away briskly through the rain.

"Really, Elketh? Fiona, too?"

Elketh turned, straightening her posture even though her thigh muscles were like jelly. "What are you doing here?"

"Looking for you," her younger brother said. Owain had a bad habit of being able to find Elketh, no matter where on the island she might be hiding. "It's time. Father is not in a good mood."

"Already? It can't be past noon."

Owain gestured to the dark sky. "It's most certainly the evening."

"Ah, stars. All right, all right, I'm coming."

Ceridwen Hold's castle was mostly open and airy. Large windows let in plenty of light and gave the sense of being outdoors, and very few rooms were completely closed off to the outside. The castle stretched to the heavens, an asymmetrical spiral that pierced the sky, stone that reflected the sun and moon like iridescent opal. It was extravagant, and it was home, and it almost always felt like you could kiss the stars from within.

The study was one of those cut-off places. Tall, imposing, and sheltered with not even a single window. Setting foot inside was like entering a different world, an area held in abeyance wherein Elketh could only hold her breath until it was, finally, time to leave.

She found it very unsettling.

"Have a seat, Elketh," her father said from his grand oak desk.

She should have known something was wrong then; she was dripping wet, and her father would not want her on his leather chairs under normal circumstances. But she was too excited at being told the answer to a long-awaited mystery to notice.

Her father's chair was practically a throne, a plush red extravagance which stood out sharply beside the mismatched chair next to him, wherein her mother sat. The queen consort Gwenhwyfar was radiant—Elketh liked to think she inherited that from her mother—in a midnight-blue dress trimmed in silver that set off her deep brown skin. Her mother took in Elketh's state—rain-soaked in her riding clothes—with a raised eyebrow.

Elketh's bottom squelched as she took her seat. She had to hold her knees in her hands to stop them from bouncing.

"I don't suppose you can have Isolde send for a fresh dress," her father said to her mother, as though Elketh were not there at all.

"I'll have it done at once."

Elketh cleared her throat. "What am I dressing up for at this hour?"

The king scratched out something with a quill pen onto paper. He liked to look busy, as though you weren't worth his time, Elketh always thought. "You are meeting the new consort tonight," he said.

Unusual. Nobody had told Elketh things would move along so fast. "Oh. I see."

"Do you?" he asked.

She raised her gaze to his, answering the challenge. "Who is she?"

"A princess."

In her head, Elketh pumped her fist. "Of Olwen?"

"Of Torden."

Torden? Elketh racked her brain but couldn't imagine the place. She had guessed her father would set her up with someone else from the Elven Islands; they squabbled with one another regularly, and could always use the stability that came with a marriage alliance. The long lifespans of elves made the opportunity to cement marriage alliances rare. "I confess, Father, I do not know Torden."

Alarm bells rang in Elketh's head when she noticed the pained look on her mother's face. "You do know Torden, honey."

Elketh bit her lip. Sure, geography wasn't her strongest subject, but she was positive she hadn't missed something like an entire country. Unless it was a very small country. Oh, stars, maybe even on the continent. She had no desire to spend fifty days with the consort's family on the continent.

"Torden and Lynby have been tense for some years," said King Gareth, "as you know. I have made an agreement with Torden to give them our army as a military ally. A preventative measure against the numerous warlords of Lynby, if they were ever to strike."

She did not know either of those names.

"Elketh, sweetheart..." Her mother glanced at her father. "Torden is just over the channel."

"I apologize. I didn't realize there were any elf countries right over the channel." Over the channel was pure orc country, or so Elketh thought. The nearest elven settlements outside of their little island cluster were far south.

"There aren't," the king said curtly. "Your betrothed is Princess Ruga of Torden. We will head there tonight to celebrate the union over a feast they are kind enough to host."

"Princess Ruga?" She did not even like the way it sounded in her mouth, the harsh G and the long vowel. "We're going tonight? How long have you known?"

Her father did not deign to give her an answer. Instead, he patted the back of his wife's hand, dismissing both of them. Obediently, Elketh followed her mother out of the room, but her mother refused to answer any of her questions. "Isolde will pick out a new dress for you. Be ready to leave in fifteen minutes."

Fifteen minutes was nothing; it took Elketh just ten minutes to get up to her room with all the castle stairs. She rushed as best as she could up the winding staircase with her legs still worn out, but stopped when she spotted Owain descending the stairs.

"What is happening?" he asked when he saw her. "Father said we're traveling tonight."

"Oh, Owain, where in the world is Torden?"

Owain's face twisted at the name. "Why would we be going there?"

"That's... I'm engaged to Princess Ruga."

"The orc princess?" Owain asked, and Elketh's throat dropped into her stomach.

"Torden is an orc country," she said. She remembered that, now. Or maybe she had been in denial. It was not a place she thought of often because she had so little to do with orcs and did not particularly care for their affairs or politics.

They had to be fucking kidding her.

CHAPTER TWO

Princess Ruga Karrsdaughter watched with apprehension from the shore as the elvish procession approached by ferry.

It was unusual for a group of elves to come at once; they made her uneasy. The only elves that frequently visited Torden in packs were traders, and, just the one time, she'd seen the messengers that delivered the marriage proposal for Torden to ally itself with Branwen. A proposal that Ruga's sister, Queen Astrid, said yes to before considering that the orc throne was not obtained through blood lineage. And as a princess but not an heir, Ruga herself was the best choice for the elves' consort, even if it meant living out the rest of her life on an elf island rather than the land she called home. The arrangement was strange to many of Torden's citizens, Ruga knew. No orc country had ever cemented a political relationship via marriage alliance.

She snuck a look at her sister, standing regally and almost unnaturally still, and gleaned nothing from her stance.

The other orcs were getting restless, as were the horses they often provided the elves in exchange for their island goods. Ruga had no doubt that everyone was very hungry, and that in the castle kitchens, the chefs were working overtime to keep the food warm without drying it out. Technically, the elves were late, but if stereotypes were to be believed, Branwen's elves did everything on their own time.

King Gareth was unmistakable as the ferry came closer. His elaborate crown glinted with light from the elves' torches. At his side, his queen whispered something into his ear.

Ruga found it hard to determine which of the elves was her betrothed.

She'd obsessed for weeks over her sister's suggestion that she supply the elves a short biography of herself. Every night before she went to bed, she crossed out lines and crumpled ruined paper as she tried to come up with a list of her accomplishments and skills—a list that was accurate but not conceited, adequately conveying her appeal as a wife and what she could contribute to the elvish court. When Ruga handed the note to their messenger, perspiring profusely, she sent up a prayer to the goddess that the elves wouldn't retract the much-needed support over poor word choice.

The elves sent back a note, ripped off from another piece of paper, that declared the elvish princess "looked a lot like the king" and enjoyed archery. At its best, it was uninformative. At its worst, it was insulting.

The elves were here now, tumbling onto the shore. There was a shifting of leather greaves as the orc guard of Torden straightened themselves. During wartime, the queen's félag wore metal armor; the leather was half ornamental.

The king thrust a somewhat damp-looking elf in a cobalt blue dress forward. "My daughter, Elketh."

Ruga stepped forward and dipped her head. She couldn't help but think that the elf she was to marry looked fragile, breakable.

Elketh was tall and thin, and she seemed to sway in the breeze, as though a puff of air could knock her off-balance. Against all logic, Ruga slouched her shoulders to make herself smaller. "Greetings, Your Highness. I am Princess Ruga."

The elf's dark eyes darted up to meet hers and then quickly away. She hooked her hair—hair so dark it was almost blue, stretching down to the middle of her back, slightly frizzy from the humidity—around one ear.

"We have prepared a feast for your retinue," Ruga's sister said, her strong voice carrying over the perhaps too-large gap between the elves and the orcs. "If you follow us, we'll show you the way to the great hall."

"Lead on," said King Gareth.

It was an incredibly awkward march back to the castle.

The smell of spiced foods hit Ruga before anything else as they entered the feast hall. The hall was usually homey, bringing to mind memories of long nights toasty by the fire, dining and drinking and sharing joy with the people Ruga cared about most. Dirt floors tamped down by many footprints, warm walls adorned only by a few tapestries, and three long, pockmarked tables with bench seats on either side where the inhabitants of Vakker Castle could sit elbow-to-elbow.

Tonight, the hall was more beautifully adorned as if to show off to the elves that orcs could be sophisticated, too. The orcs assumed elves were used to frippery that orcs sometimes went without. This equated to candles everywhere, in addition to the already-cozy hearth in the center, and lace adornments on everything. Ruga and other orcs skilled in lacework had spent the last few months laboring in preparation even though everything would likely be stained and splotched with grease by the end of the night.

Ruga did not miss the sneer on the elf king's face when he entered the room, and she couldn't help but feel like she'd wasted hours of her life. She took her seat on the end of the bench next to Astrid's throne; the elf king sat on the other side, where the captain of the queen's félag, Hedda, usually sat, and his wife next to him. A guard wiped the bench space next to Ruga for the elvish princess, and Ruga tried not to stare as Elketh settled into it, delicate as a flower.

The food was brought out immediately, as though the staff couldn't wait another minute. The chefs had put everything they had into this meal—there were aromatic platters of pork porridge, steaming loaves of sourdough, and aesthetically pleasing arrangements of fruits imported from the Elven Islands, for something familiar. Bowls of berries and cashews complimented platters of boiled herring. Ruga loaded her plate with grains, fruits, and nuts as the elves sat still as stones, watching.

Maybe it wasn't to their liking. Queen Astrid had done research on elvish appetites and found them to be not so different from orcish ones. She'd ordered the kitchens to prepare dishes from both cultures for adventurous and picky eaters alike.

"We serve ourselves?" the elf queen asked in a quiet voice.

"My apologies, Your Majesty," Astrid said from her seat. Her plate was loaded twice as high as anyone else's. "We take what we like from the communal platters."

The elves started to load their plates, too, and a collective breath was released into the room. Tension ebbed and flowed like the mead in their goblets.

Fifty days. That was what she'd been told was elvish tradition for familiarizing oneself with an arranged partner prior to marriage. The response to Ruga's attempt to inform the elves about herself didn't seem to suit this custom well.

She really, really wished that the fifty days of the elvish princess being here would bring them closer together, rather than being as tense as this dinner.

King Gareth and Queen Gwenhwyfar shared pleasantries with Ruga and Astrid nicely enough, but Princess Elketh said nothing. She ate her soup as austerely as a priestess from the temple. Ruga stole a glance at Elketh's plate and saw a hand with smooth, well-cared for cuticles, but on Elketh's forearm, she noticed a scar, like the elvish princess had been in a tussle. The princess was more athletic than Ruga thought from afar, too, the muscles in her arm flexing whenever she ladled her spoon back into the soup for another tiny sip.

When the blackberry mead was served, Elketh had much of it. Ruga heard that elves drank watered-down wine, but mead went down easy as water even when it was far more potent. She hoped Elketh knew that, and thought to warn her, but didn't want to be overbearing. Elketh was an adult; she would know how much she could drink and stay seemly.

Dessert was brought out—pastries tantalizingly drizzled with honey. Ruga dug into hers with gusto; she loved sweet things, and honey especially. She sat back with sticky fingers as Astrid laughed at a joke King Gareth shared.

There was a scraping noise, louder than the din of the dining room, as Elketh nudged her plate away from her with a single finger, stopping not in the center of the table but continuing until it crashed into the elvish queen's plate across from her. The entire room flinched as the pottery made contact.

For just a moment, King Gareth glared daggers at his daughter, who demurely set her hands in her lap. Ruga watched the interaction with interest but told herself not to overanalyze them. It seemed like the king was a strict father, and maybe Elketh was used to a rigid environment. Ruga could help the elf princess feel more at ease.

Subtly, Ruga shifted toward Elketh. The elf smelled nice, a combination of rain water and the blackberry mead she'd been consuming by the gallon. Ruga cleared her throat as she leaned even closer. "I'm looking forward to getting to know you better," she said.

Next to her, the elf princess stiffened. She picked up her goblet in one of her pretty hands and finished it off, already reaching for the pitcher to refill it. Bright liquid sloshed over the sides of the goblet as she poured rather drunkenly. "Princess Ruga," Elketh said, the name like a curse between her violet-stained teeth, "I would do *anything* to escape this place."

So Elketh had a dry sense of humor. Ruga could appreciate that. She laughed under her breath, loud enough for Elketh to hear but not so loud it would draw attention from everyone else's revelry.

The vehemence in Elketh's eyes sparkled so intensely that Ruga's mouth slammed closed with a distinct clicking of her tusks. If Elketh learned the glare from her father, she had certainly improved upon it.

The elf wasn't joking. She didn't want to be there.

Panic fluttered in Ruga's chest. She was supposed to marry this woman, but it looked more like she would get strangled in her sleep.

Perhaps Princess Elketh was not so breakable as she first thought.

CHAPTER THREE

There was no way Elketh was going to marry an orc princess. It was preposterous. Absurd. The fact that her father even entertained the idea was deeply insulting. He meant to throw her away. How would she ever be taken seriously on Branwen if she brought back an orc bride? All of the other respectable countries had elf consorts. Cementing the alliances between the Elven Islands was too important to throw away an important princess like Elketh on an alliance from the *continent*.

Elketh tried to excuse herself from the dinner early. She stood from the bench—unhygienic, that they all had to sit so close together and not in separate chairs—and boldly proclaimed that she had a headache. Her mother had the audacity to roll her eyes at Elketh, who often claimed a headache at events she did not care to attend. Instead of being escorted to whatever rooms they had for her by a servant, where she could pretend to go to bed and then stow herself away on the ferry until it returned to Branwen, the orc princess herself offered to take her.

Elketh absolutely hated chivalry.

The orc princess walked ahead of her, perhaps understanding by the threatening tone Elketh used earlier that she was not in the mood to be friendly. For some unknown reason, the orcs dined in a great hall separate from their castle, which annoyed Elketh for being impractical. Princess Ruga pointed out rooms as she walked—the library, the kitchens, the scullery, the meadery, the aviary, the armory.

Despite herself, Elketh couldn't help but admire the orc princess's figure from behind. Though the orc wore a delicately patterned dress, her biceps bulged at the fabric. Wistfully, Elketh was reminded of Rhiannon and the marriage she'd dreamt of. She thought of Rhiannon's toned body, hauling wood for no reason other than to show off her muscles.

Elketh was a big fan of toned women.

Ruga was not Rhiannon. Elketh found her intriguing, though. More than she expected to. Horns like a ram's curled around either side of Ruga's purplish hair, and whenever Ruga turned, Elketh noted the two cute tusks that jutted over a very soft-looking top lip. Without the horns, Elketh was almost the same height as the orc, which she had not expected. She was told that orcs were eight, nine feet tall. She was also told that they were green, though that didn't seem to be the case; Ruga's skin was as naturally brown as Elketh's. The only odd thing about her was her hair, which had a purplish tint. Elvish hair did not come in that unnatural color. Perhaps Ruga dyed hers artificially.

Elketh was less comfortable with the dismantling of her preconceived notions—with acknowledging she'd been *lied* to—than accepting that Ruga was so normal in appearance. Pretty, even.

Ruga led Elketh up a flight of narrow stairs and stopped at a door. "This is where you'll be staying. It's—"

"Great," Elketh said without preamble, and turned the handle herself. She began to shut the door behind her, but the crafty orc stuck a foot between the door and the wall. It was very impressive that Ruga only winced when Elketh tried to slam the door in her face anyway.

"Princess Elketh... These are my rooms also. We are supposed to share them."

"What kind of hospitality is that? Do you not have rooms to put up guests?"

Ruga's eye was the only thing Elketh could see through the crack. "We are to be wed. Please do not lock me out of my own rooms."

Huffing, Elketh stormed away from the door.

The room was nothing to write home about. Elketh's apartments at home were exactly how she liked them, decorated with furs from her hunts, gifts from her suitors, art and armor commissioned from local craftspeople. This bedchamber was bland as a temple, its only adornments an entire wall of chainmail, a smallish bookcase, a simple wardrobe, and a writing desk and chair. The bed looked soft, at least.

How silly, for Elketh to note the comfort of the bed. She did not intend to stay. Longingly, she gauged the dimensions of the singular window.

"Elketh," the orc said, and Elketh flinched at the use of her name without its title, "I confess that I'm confused. Why would you agree to the betrothal if you did not want to be here?"

"I did not agree to anything," Elketh said, crossing her arms. She leaned against the overly plain desk. "I only found out today that *you're* my bride. I had no say in it at all."

The orc's mouth formed such a perfectly surprised "O" that Elketh almost apologized for her bad attitude. Almost. "Didn't you get my letter?" Ruga asked.

"What fucking letter?"

Ruga sat at the end of her bed, looking dazed. "You're not here of your own volition?"

"Of course I'm not. Do I look like I'm here of my own volition?" Elketh spat.

Knowing she was being petty, Elketh mussed up the papers on Ruga's desk, hoping whatever she ruined at least minorly inconvenienced the orc. She removed the quill from its well, praying it would be dry the next time Ruga tried to write one of those alleged letters.

"This must be some sort of mistake," Ruga said from the bed.

There was something off about the look of the orc. At dinner—at least until Elketh had told her about wanting to leave—the orc had been relaxed, enjoying her meal enthusiastically. Now, she exuded defeat.

"There's no mistake." Elketh approached Ruga, and the orc leaned back as though facing down an enemy. "My father arranged this whole thing. He only told me today because he *knew* I would try to get out of it." The elvish king had no reason to involve himself in orcish politics.

"We would never keep you in Vakker Castle against your will, Elketh. I hope you know that."

Elketh realized the orc was uncomfortably close to her face. She snatched her hand away as Ruga reached for it. Up close, Ruga was even more surprising. Her neck was muscular, too, cords shifting under the skin moving as she spoke. There was an undeniable earnestness in her gaze that made Elketh's stomach swirl unpleasantly. "Prove it," Elketh said, turning away.

"I'll go find my sister and explain the, ah, misunderstanding." Ruga rose from the bed. "I'm sure we can clear this up."

"The only way this can be cleared up is if it means I'll be asleep in my bed by tomorrow."

"Of course, Princess Elketh. My sincerest apologies for the mistake. I'll get this fixed." The orc stopped at the door and glanced back at Elketh. "I promise."

And then she was gone.

Was she really going to fight for Elketh's say in the marriage? It sounded too good to be true. Elketh had just met Ruga today; she wasn't ready to trust her just yet. Still, Ruga wasn't what she expected. Not at all. She almost felt guilty for her getaway plans.

Almost.

She popped her head out the door. There was someone in the hallway, dressed in armor, unmoving. A soldier, guarding her.

Shit.

Elketh dumped blankets onto the floor. In books, heroines climbed out the window by stripping sheets and tying them together. She made sure the window opened first and then selected the thinnest sheet from the pile.

It would not rip no matter how hard she tried. The sheet may as well have been made of iron. Her fingers ached as they clutched at the fabric until she was out of breath, and the sheet was in the same state as it had been when she started. Maybe stretched out a little.

Well, fine. They were only on the second floor, not the top of some tower. Elketh would just tie the sheet to a bed post and dangle it out the window, climb down as far as she could, and then jump down the rest of the way.

Elketh began the laborious task of pushing the bed as close as she could to the window. It was incredibly heavy. She had to move the wardrobe and a very tall, very well-stuffed bookshelf out of the way first to make room for it.

The bed was just a yard or so from the window when the doorknob turned.

This night was not going how Elketh thought it would. She shoved the sheet under the bed just before Ruga opened the door again.

"I can't find the elves," Ruga said. She stepped into the room and froze. "What are you doing? Why is my bedspread on the floor? What's with—"

"I was rearranging in case I had to stay," Elketh blurted. "I hate what you've done with the place. And I like to sleep on the floor."

Ruga took in the mess and shook her head as though brushing it off. "I'm pretty sure my sister is having a private conversation with your king somewhere. I couldn't find them, though, and there don't seem to be any elves lingering in the dining hall. What would you like me to do, Princess? Should we wait for morning?"

The elves would be gone by morning. Even if the orc queen offered them hospitality, they wouldn't want to stay in orc country for longer than they had to, and certainly not overnight. The fact that Ruga hadn't seen any of them... The elves were likely boarding the ferry as they spoke.

The only thing Elketh could do was scheme. If she got rid of Ruga, she could still stow herself on the ferry.

"That is a shame," Elketh said carefully. Easy. Her brother always said she played it up a little too much when she wanted something—she usually had time to rehearse. "A real shame. I guess we can deal with it in the morning. I'm so tired, you know? I think I'll go to bed."

She waited for Ruga to leave.

Ruga did not make any move to do so.

"All right," Ruga said. "I should go to bed, too."

Oh, stars. The orc was going to stay.

"I'm not very comfortable with that. I prefer sleeping alone." Inherently untrue.

"You will be sleeping alone," the orc said, "since you like to sleep on the floor. I'll just sleep in my bed as I always do. Take as many blankets as you need."

Damn this courteous monster. "Is there any chance I can get my own quarters, just for the night?" Elketh asked, desperate. "I'm having a case of...diarrhea."

"Uh..." The orc scratched the back of her head. "Well, all right. I'll find somewhere else to sleep tonight. You can...just...stay here."

"Thank you very much, Princess Ruga." Oh, and her manners. Elketh was always forgetting her manners. "And thank you for your *wonderful* hospitality."

Ruga looked flummoxed as she left the room a second time.

Hands scrabbling, Elketh extracted the sheet from its hiding spot and yanked the bed toward the window with every ounce of stress-induced strength she had.

CHAPTER FOUR

A hundred times, Ruga imagined how this night would go. She was a practical orc—she played out how it could succeed, and projected what things could go wrong.

In all her imagining, she never thought it could be quite this bad.

The elf princess did not want to be there and hardly knew about her at all. Ruga mourned the time and effort she put into crafting the letter that was supposed to endear her to the princess, the one Elketh clearly never received. The elf king was some sort of schemer.

As a result, not only were the preparations for the arrangement gone to waste—and this did stress Ruga a great deal—but a hollow disappointment had bloomed in her chest at the thought of the marriage not going through. Admittedly, Ruga had allowed herself to daydream about what Elketh might be like. How Ruga planned to enchant her with Vakker Castle and its bustling town. The way Ruga would court Elketh and make her feel wanted in spite of the odd circumstances. How they might actually fall in love.

Ruga's hopes had been dashed against the floor like her bedsheets.

And that was before she considered the complications Elketh's refusal would bring up for Astrid. It worried Ruga that her sister was nowhere to be found. Surely, Astrid would not have agreed to the betrothal if she knew one of the parties was unwilling.

The problem with letting Elketh stay in Ruga's rooms was that Ruga had nowhere to sleep. While the castle had unoccupied apartments, there was a guard in each hallway, and Ruga had no doubt that they would question the motives of Ruga's bride-to-be if Ruga went and found another resting spot. The last thing Ruga wanted was to embarrass her sister without discussing a course of action first. Arranged marriage was already fairly unprecedented; an arranged marriage to an unwilling party was both absurd and immoral.

Ruga tried her sister's door one last time, and then the room where she sometimes met with advisors and visiting orcs from across Torden. Maybe she had left the castle completely, to escort the elves back to the ferry and ensure safe passage.

After searching, Ruga could confirm there were absolutely no elves in the castle save for the librarian. It seemed that Ruga's bad feeling about Elketh's father was correct—the king had left Elketh here and hightailed it back to Branwen. It was spineless, and it left a bad taste in Ruga's mouth. She wondered if her sister would do anything about the deceptive nature of the whole thing, whether it would be called off completely.

At least Elketh would get what she wanted. Sure, the marriage not happening was disappointing, but Ruga had to prioritize the elf's safety over her own tumultuous feelings.

Ruga cleared her throat at the library doors. The librarian—Vera—looked up from what she was writing in a journal. She had deep red hair, her elf ears poking out of it on either side of her head, and pale, freckled skin. Her nose wrinkled when she saw Ruga.

Generally, the two got along, and Ruga was pretty sure she was one of the few people who had garnered Vera's respect. But Vera was close to the queen's handmaiden. They'd come to Vakker Castle together nearly a decade ago. Anything Ruga said to her—or within earshot of her—was likely to be passed along. Ruga rarely had anything to hide, but she still found herself making their conversations short and tense.

"Ruga," Vera said. "How can I help you?"

"Have you seen my sister?"

The elf grunted, nodding her head toward the back of the library. Astrid had a nook she liked to escape to when the pressure of being queen became too much. She was adamant about not being disturbed when hiding out at the library, but desperate times, and all that.

Ruga turned the corner and gently knocked on the side of a bookcase. She stifled laughter—Astrid had her head back in a chair, a book open over her face, and when Ruga knocked, Astrid jolted, and the book collapsed into her lap in a mess of pages. Behind her, Astrid's ever-watchful human handmaiden, Freya, leaned against a bookshelf looking quietly amused.

Astrid reached for her crown, set delicately on a side table, but stopped when she saw it was Ruga disturbing her. After fifty-two years of rule, the queen still held fast to the idea that always wearing the crown in front of her subjects was essential, especially after the orcs of Lynby seceded, further dividing Torden. Anything she could do to cement her authority, she would try.

"What's the matter? You look like someone died," the queen said.

"Are the elves gone?"

"Yes. Their king said he had things to do tonight." Astrid yawned into her bejeweled hand. She was a bit taller than Ruga and certainly too big for her chair, her legs splayed out in her trousers. "I think he didn't want to be here longer than he had to."

"The elf princess is unwilling to marry me," Ruga said. "She only found out about the arrangement today."

Astrid was quiet. She rubbed a bit of dried drool off the corner of her mouth. "That's unexpected."

"What should we do?"

"Does anyone else know?"

The worst thing about being the sister of royalty was keeping up appearances. "No, not yet. She doesn't like the idea of sharing a room with me, though."

The orc queen sighed. "I should have known it was too good to be true. How embarrassing for us." She was angry, Ruga could tell, from the twitch of her brow. Astrid was always good at hiding her emotions, but she was a bit looser about them in front of Ruga. "That son of a—"

"Can we send the ferry back out to the island when it returns?" If they did, Ruga would get to sleep in her own bed.

Astrid straightened herself in the chair. "We'd better ask permission first. I wouldn't want the elf to be stranded if the king doesn't want her there. Who knows what he was thinking, dumping her here...?"

Nudging Astrid's arm out of the way, Ruga settled herself on the arm of the chair.

"And," Astrid said, "maybe don't let anyone know about this until I've sorted it out. I'll have Freya consult Brenn. Maybe the seer knows something. What a headache."

A headache indeed. Not only had Ruga made physical and mental preparations, she'd made personal sacrifices. She pushed down frustration at the elf king's carelessness.

"Do you have somewhere to sleep?" Astrid lifted herself from the chair, playfully shoving Ruga out of the way as she did.

"Yes," Ruga lied.

Vakker Castle was full of empty rooms. Ruga tried one at the end of a long hall first, which she knew to be unoccupied, but just as she was opening the door, a guard stopped her, kindly inquiring as to what she was doing there and whether she needed help. She made up an excuse and scurried away, not wanting even the queen's trusted félag to know of this embarrassment, but the next room she tried was the same, and the next, and the next.

There were a lot of things people could say about Queen Astrid, but no one could say that her félag wasn't loyal and well-staffed.

With nowhere else to go, Ruga resigned herself to sleep in her favorite place in the world: her rose garden.

The rose garden was small, but it was a good place to think, and a better place for enjoying solitude in what could often be a hectic court. It was gated off. All the roses were white, blooming in beautiful patches, the buds reflecting the moonlight, carefully cultivated by Ruga herself. The roses were her favorite hobby.

She sat on the ornate stone bench in the center of the garden. It was warm tonight, at least, the time between spring and summer when temperatures were not yet too hot. Of course, Ruga had forgotten to grab a blanket in all the stress of the Elketh situation.

How odd, that the elf had thrown everything on the floor and tried to rearrange the room the second Ruga left. Were all of Branwen's elves that particular, or just Elketh? Maybe it wouldn't even matter soon, if the elf was to go back. Ruga might not see her again after the next morning.

Ruga settled herself into the grass with her head just shaded under the bench so it wouldn't be completely blinding when the sun rose. It was comfortable enough, if a bit damp. She would have liked to change into her bedclothes, too, but they were in her room with Elketh. She closed her eyes, and breathed in the smell of her flowers, and imagined the waves of the sea lapping on Torden's shore.

There was a grunting noise above her. Some kind of animal in a tree, perhaps. Ruga shifted onto her side and imagined the waves some more.

The animal yelped, followed by a crashing noise.

Ruga got up so fast she almost brained herself on the edge of the bench. "Hello?" she called out. Astrid told her to keep a guard around at all times, what with the fraught political environment, but of course Ruga hadn't wanted a guard to know about Elketh's reluctance. Stars, she might be paying for that now.

As she stood, Ruga brushed mud off her backside and picked bits of grass from her hair. A flutter of movement caught her eye from the window above. The rose garden was just at the ground below her rooms, so she could admire her roses from afar when she didn't have time to spend with them. Ruga's heart pounded when she realized what the fluttering was: one of her bedsheets.

The elf princess had *escaped.*

CHAPTER FIVE

Elketh stumbled as she ran from the orc castle as fast as she could. Her hand throbbed; she'd nearly fallen into a tree and had grabbed a branch as she went, so it was bleeding, and not just a little. The cloak she'd found to obscure herself was one of Ruga's, a thick beast of a thing that left way too much room for horns Elketh definitely didn't have. In an ideal world, nobody would notice the lack of horns in the dark before she reached the ferry.

Rage fueled Elketh as she sighted the wharf where the ferry had dropped her off. How *dare* her father abandon her here, leaving her at the whims of these orcs? He had no idea what they were capable of. She would get there before the ferry left, and then he would owe her big time. She wasn't getting married to anyone, at all, for her entire reign. She could rule just fine on her own.

There were lanterns along the wharf, and Elketh set for them at full speed, sweating through the thick cloak on the temperate night. Her brain caught on slower than her body as she skidded to a halt, so out of breath that she felt like her lungs might expand right out of her torso. Elketh held her knees, panting, at the edge of the pier.

She could see the ferry. It was far away, almost to the outline of the island of Branwen already.

They had really left without her.

Her father had abandoned her here, probably the second she excused herself from dinner. She knew why. He knew she would never agree to this, and leaving her stranded meant forcing her to talk to the orcs and learn their customs and, eventually, come around to the idea of marrying one of them. Elketh knew this because she had much in common with her father.

Unfortunately for him, that included her stubbornness.

Elketh took several steadying breaths and stood, her scheming mind already calculating. All the boats at the wharf were moored, and only a couple could be rowed by a single person. She headed for one of the smaller fishing boats. She could row, but she was terrible with knots, and she fiddled with the one connected to the little boat with difficulty.

Rope burn aggravated her bleeding hand. She smeared blood all over the rope in her panic when she heard the rush of approaching footsteps.

"Princess!" the damned orc princess called.

Screaming in frustration, Elketh dropped the rope. She rushed back to the pier as the orc approached and ran to where the planks jutted over the water.

"We can sort this out," the orc said. She was at the intersection of the pier and wharf now, reaching one hand out to Elketh. Her silky purple hair was in disarray, her dress muddy. A vine twined around one of her horns.

And there was earnestness in her eyes, an openness of her expression. Elketh screamed again; it echoed off of the water. "He left! Do you see that?"

"Yes, and I'm terribly, terribly sorry. Please come back so we can deal with this diplomatically. If we handle it wrong, Torden may call war on your king for a fake proposal, or your people on us for..." Ruga trailed off, swallowing.

For kidnapping her. That was what she'd been about to say.

Elketh then saw the engagement in a whole new light. Not only had her father dumped her here and left her stranded, but he'd also set Elketh up so that if she defied the marriage arrangement, her refusal would cause a literal war. He was banking on Elketh not wanting to start a war between Branwen and Torden. It was a bold move. A bold enough move that Elketh was suddenly positive the orcs would also force her to stay to avoid conflict.

"You can't keep me here," Elketh spat at the orc. "You won't take me alive."

"Are you serious?" the orc asked. To her credit, she did look bewildered. "We would never do anything to harm—"

Elketh didn't hear the rest of the sentence. She was too busy jumping into the harbor.

Her breaststroke was strong, and she was still young, less than three hundred years old. It wouldn't be easy, but she could make it to the island, or at least dawdle enough for Ruga to realize she wasn't coming back and leave so she could steal that boat.

The cloak was made up of so much fabric, though.

It weighed her down. She cursed herself for not discarding it sooner, and tried to shuffle it off, but the sleeves were heavy, and it was getting mangled, and the sea was neither calm nor warm.

Elketh didn't know which way was up. Only that the cloak was keeping her captive the way Ruga had. She fought it, kicking and punching, but it wouldn't loosen its hold on her. Water burned as it went down her throat.

There was a splash, a movement in the water that propelled Elketh downward. A firm arm around her middle. Then she was being dragged, hauled upwards, and the warmth of the night air kissed her face again. Elketh coughed, sputtering, and elbowed her captor in the gut.

"Stars, will you stop?" the orc hissed in her ear. "What's the matter with you?"

Elketh fought her more, but the orc had her in her grasp tightly. The orc swung herself back up onto the pier with one hand, Elketh in the other, and dumped Elketh onto the wood. Water left Elketh's lungs in a burst when her back collided with the boards of the pier. She was spent. She couldn't do anything other than try to get her breath back.

The orc was so strong. Elketh could hardly believe Ruga had dragged her kicking and screaming out of the water.

"Have you calmed down yet?" Ruga asked. She leaned over Elketh, hair dripping water. Her eyelashes were damp and clumped together.

Pitifully, Elketh coughed again. So much for all the mead she'd consumed earlier; there was no residual alcohol-induced pleasantness left at all. Elketh desperately wanted to be so inebriated that the entire world was a blur. She thought of her favorite tavern back at Branwen with its beautiful women and better drink.

They had to have places to drink in Torden, too.

"I am," she said, mostly to herself, "tragically sober."

"Excuse me?" Despite her confusion, Ruga reached out to help Elketh up. Elketh grabbed the orc's forearm to lift herself from the pier.

"I said, I'm tragically sober. There was a tavern around here, wasn't there? I think we passed it..." And then she was off, leaving the orc behind. Hopefully, Ruga was too overwhelmed by everything to follow her.

There would be no such luck. The unmistakable wet squish of Ruga's shoes followed her to the tavern.

CHAPTER SIX

This elf couldn't be a legitimate match; the Branwen king had sent her knowing she would humiliate Torden.

Ruga watched as Elketh traversed down the main road, squinting into dark shopfronts, tracking down a tavern. Ruga was deeply uncomfortable. She sure wasn't going to help Elketh reach any public destination. It was bad enough that Ruga had left the castle without telling her sister. Now, they could be seen and gossiped about.

One of Elketh's talents appeared to be locating sources of alcohol. Victoriously, she swung open the door of a tavern and made herself comfortable at a long table that already had several orcs seated on the end. The tavern was warm and crowded, smelling of yeast and the sweaty bodies of Astrid's off-duty guards.

"Give me that cloak," Ruga said self-consciously.

Elketh ignored her. "Barmaid! Bring me something strong!"

Frustrated at being snubbed, Ruga entered Elketh's personal space and undid the cloak's clasp herself, using it to shield her body from the prying eyes of guards that had very clearly noticed her already. This was easily one of the longest nights of her life, and it seemed only destined to get longer. "Elketh..."

"What?" The barmaid had brought over a giant stein of frothy ale in spite of the rude nature of Elketh's request. "Do you want one?" Elketh asked Ruga.

"I shouldn't."

"She'll take one, too," Elketh told the barmaid. She turned her pretty elvish eyes on Ruga, then, and Ruga felt her face get warm.

"I'll be right back." Ruga knew the owner. She found the back room and convinced him to give her two clean cloths and a vial of clear liquor. When she returned to the table, she almost wished she hadn't bothered.

Elketh's smile was malicious, the tilt of her chin cocky. "So, Ruga. Tell me why you're so determined to keep me as your prisoner." Her voice was a little hoarse from nearly drowning.

Without answering, Ruga gestured for Elketh to give her the hand that she'd injured. A blank expression on her face, the elf let Ruga rub an alcohol-soaked rag over her wound as though she didn't feel the pain. Princess Elketh downed ale with her free hand as she watched Ruga work.

Over and over, Ruga imagined the moment that Elketh had looked her dead in the eye and then leaped into the sea. It was absurd. Had the elf really meant to swim all the way back to the island? Or had she anticipated that Ruga would jump in to save her as a sort of test? What kind of person would do that?

Ruga got the impression Elketh was used to people doing things for her. She was someone used to getting anything she wanted, and if she didn't, she would go so far as to nearly kill herself to get it anyway.

Securely, Ruga wrapped the injury with the second cloth. Whenever the elf did return to her people, Ruga didn't want them to think the orcs had hurt her.

"Are you going to answer my question? Are you stupid?"

Ruga batted Elketh's hand, waving in front of her face, away. "We aren't keeping you captive. This was supposed to be a mutual agreement."

The elf took another deep drag of ale. The froth lined her full lips when she set it back down. Ruga tried very hard not to stare as Elketh licked it away. Even bedraggled as she was, Elketh was something of a beauty, willowy and majestic from afar with an underlying muscle you only noticed up close. The archery, perhaps. That was the only thing Ruga had been allowed to know about her before she arrived. She didn't even know if it was true that Elketh liked archery, or if someone had made it up.

"Well. It was not mutual."

"I see that," Ruga conceded.

"I would like to go home. What's your ransom? How much will it take to buy you off?"

"Ransom?"

A look around the room revealed that Elketh had garnered the attention of several of the orcs. There were other elves here, though only a few, and they were known around town.

"We aren't keeping you here against your will." Gingerly, Ruga set her hand over Elketh's on the table right as her stein arrived. "I hope you know that we would never try to trick you. I thought that we were going to be married. To ally our countries."

Gently, Elketh removed her hand from under Ruga's. There was a conflicted look on her face that only injured Ruga a little bit. To the orcs, Ruga was a catch—that is to say, she hadn't been unlucky when it came to romance. But to this elf with her delicate features, Ruga was ugly, monstrous, a thing with horns and sharp teeth. It was like looking in warped glass, to try to see herself through Elketh's eyes.

"I spoke with my sister the queen," Ruga added, when the silence became uncomfortable. "She said we would petition your father for your return in the morning. She was not fond of the trickery, either. We were both under the impression that you knew and consented to the arrangement."

Elketh adopted Ruga's ale as her own. "I'm not sure what to think. I don't know if I believe you."

"I don't care whether you believe me or not. If you don't mind," Ruga said shortly, "I would prefer sending you back home on the ferry, knowing your father wants you there, rather than you swimming your way back."

The corners of Elketh's mouth turned up. Her expression was disarmingly winsome. "I'll stay until we hear from him, as long as I can be shit-faced the whole time."

Ruga was never going to hear the end of this from her sister. She should have towed Elketh back to the castle against her will and let herself be the villain. Better that than to undermine the queen. Ruga could only imagine the things people would say about the elf princess—it was very obvious who she was. The queen had a fairly loyal group within her félag, but any random orc in here could be seething with the same resentment the Lynby orcs bore for Astrid. The last thing they needed was for the queen to look weak, like she couldn't control a single elf.

Ruga put her head in her hands. The sooner this was over with, the better.

"Do you promise?" Elketh asked quietly from across the table.

Ruga lifted her head. "Promise what?"

"That you'll send a letter to my father in the morning?"

The end of Elketh's nose was pinkish. Oh, stars, she was crying.

"Of course," Ruga said, soothingly. "I'll have a messenger go out first thing."

Elketh nodded, staring morosely into her second empty stein like it held the answers to her problems. "And what happens if I'm not allowed to go back?"

"What—ah—do you think he won't allow you?" What *would* happen if she wasn't allowed back? They could offer her a spot at the castle, or maybe a vocation, but Ruga got the impression Elketh was unused to labor.

"No, I think he will," she said with a sigh. "I bet he was hoping I would just go with it. I'll be in my own bed by tomorrow afternoon."

And why don't you go with it? Ruga wanted to ask. "I see," she said, though she didn't. She'd suffered losses, too, for Torden's sake.

Ruga endured another stein's worth of ale in tense silence, until her shoulders began to hurt from clenching them. The elf's lucidity plummeted as she drank, muttering something about someone named Rhiannon. If this was a past lover, Ruga could empathize. She had also sacrificed love for this farce.

She pushed that thought down quickly. "We should go," Ruga said as she sent the barmaid away before Elketh could order anything else. Elketh could barely raise her head from the table as she swirled a puddle of spilled ale with one long finger, her hair draped between wooden slats. "Elketh?"

"Hmm?"

"Doesn't sleeping in a comfortable bed sound nice?"

"Mmm." Elketh began to snore.

A hand clamped over Ruga's shoulder. She flinched. It was one of the guards from the end of the table. "Do you need help taking her to the castle?" he asked. Ruga and Elketh had, actually, the attention of *all* of the queen's félag at the table, and several others from around the room. They had been watching—guarding the two—even off-duty.

"I should be able to take her," Ruga said, trying not to feel embarrassed. Astrid would definitely know about this outing by morning. Several times, she tried to lift Elketh up by the armpits, but the elf just rolled around like a ragdoll.

"Are you...sure?" the guard asked again.

"Yes," Ruga said, and hauled Elketh over her shoulder like a sack of flour.

The room was completely silent. Ruga bolted out as quick as she could without looking suspicious—as not-suspicious as you can look with someone unconscious draped over your shoulder. The tavern's patrons had the decency to wait until she reached the end of the road to laugh, but she could still hear it echoing behind her, a trail of humiliation.

CHAPTER SEVEN

It was the end of the world. Elketh had never felt like this in her life. Someone had dropped something on her head. Or maybe she didn't have a head at all anymore. Whenever she tried to roll over to lift it, her stomach roiled in an earthquake of nausea.

When she couldn't hold it in any longer, she dragged herself to the end of the bed and puked into the receptacle she kept around for occasions like these. Or she would have, if it was there. She stared at the unseemly liquid, splashed directly onto the ground, and became aware of the morning sun pummeling her entire face.

Well, that wasn't right. Elketh hated east-facing windows. She would never choose to sleep in a room with one. But there was no one else sharing this bed.

The events of last night came back to Elketh in a rush. Her hangover was not the result of a romantic escapade but the consequences of her father choosing to ally himself with the orcs.

With a groan, she pulled the blanket over her head. The orc with the muscles had promised to send a message to her father first thing in the morning. If Elketh loitered in bed as long as she could, she might only have to get up when it was time to pack her things and return home.

The sun was absurdly bright and hot even through the blanket. How did that damned orc sleep like this? Elketh tossed and turned until someone came to the door, knuckles hitting wood like explosions to Elketh's sensitive ears.

"Princess Elketh?" a voice called. It was not Ruga.

That was fast. They really had gotten ahold of her father right away. Elketh dragged herself out of the bed, one limb at a time, so slowly that the person knocked again.

It was a human. Elketh wrinkled her nose. She was not fond of humans; she did not think them worth her time, if they were only going to live for eighty years at most. How pathetic of them. "What did he say?"

"Sorry?" The human was holding a tray of breakfast food—some kind of fish stew with bread. "I've brought your breakfast."

"You don't have news from my father," Elketh said flatly.

"No, Princess. Where can I set it down?"

"On the floor." She wouldn't be able to eat it without it coming back up, anyway. "And can you draw me a bath?" Elketh was halfway back to the bed when she realized the human servant hadn't moved. "Can you draw me a bath?" she repeated, thinking maybe her gravelly voice hadn't been audible enough.

"No," the human said. Instead of putting the tray on the floor, she set it on a side table and made as if to leave.

"What kind of servant are you? Send me someone who will draw me a bath."

The servant stopped at the door. Even in her hungover haze, Elketh realized how tightly the servant gripped the handle. "I work in the *kitchens*. I am not a servant. And, kindly, most people don't have their food delivered to their rooms, but Queen Astrid said you wouldn't be in a state to dine with the rest of us." For a moment, that looked like it would be the end of it. And then the human spat on the floor, right inside the antechamber, and said, "I can see why. You look like shit."

Elketh attempted to chase the human down the hall but only made it a few steps before she was too woozy to do anything but focus on keeping herself upright.

"Are you scaring the staff off?"

Elketh jumped, nearly hitting her head against the wall. She shoved a sweaty lock of hair out of her face. "Don't sneak up on me like that. I could have killed you."

"Right. Good morning, Elketh," Ruga said. The orc was pristine, unlike how Elketh imagined she herself looked, if the servant's reaction was any indication. Ruga's purple hair was tied back in a ponytail, and she wore a yellow-orange dress with a flower pattern that complemented her skin tone, the swell of her biceps stretching the design where it met her shoulders. In the daylight, Ruga was even less intimidating; the tusks at the ends of her lips had gone from almost cute to actually cute.

Elketh thought she would puke again.

"I have something for you," Ruga said. Elketh's gaze latched onto an object in Ruga's hand: an envelope affixed with the elf king's seal.

The thought of reading any words caused another round of nausea to rock Elketh's body. She swayed lightly, grabbing for the envelope with double vision. Ruga took her hand, placing the envelope in it and letting go. The touch was completely proper.

Elketh was sick of "proper."

She tore open the seal with her teeth and dropped the envelope to the ground, holding only the thin paper of the letter. It was a very short letter, she saw without reading it.

A short letter from her father was never a good letter. He embellished his words with positive letters, enthusiastic over news that bode good fortune. With bad letters, he was economic, succinct.

Elketh,

You have two options. Bring Princess Ruga to Branwen to wed after the fifty-day engagement has passed, or do not return at all.

HRM King Gareth Ceridwen the Third

Elketh let the letter fall at her bare feet. She felt even weaker than before.

"He doesn't want you back, then?"

Elketh peered between her fingers. If she was desolate at the news, the orc's reaction was much worse. Elketh had her hands over her face so she wouldn't vomit again, but Ruga had a hand to her mouth like it was the only thing keeping her from screaming.

"No," Elketh said shortly. "He does not want me back unless it's with you."

"I won't force you to marry me," the orc said.

Even through her hangover, through the tumbling of her stomach, Elketh felt a discomfort that wasn't from drinking. It was revoltingly illogical for the orc to be *kind* to her. Over and over again, Ruga had emphasized Elketh's choice to marry or not, to stay or not. It was more than her father had given her.

"You're not what I expected," Elketh said.

"What do you mean?" Ruga asked.

Elketh was either too hungover or too embarrassed to say what she meant.

Ruga waited for an answer, and when she didn't get one, she barged into the room.

"Ex*cuse* me," Elketh said, clinging to the wall and pulling herself back into the room one hand at a time. The orc was already raiding a wardrobe. A pile of dresses was proliferating on the bed.

"It smells awful in here," Ruga said. "Didn't you see the water I left you?"

Elketh's eyes wavered to the other side of the bed. There was, indeed, water sitting there in a fancy pitcher, but Elketh had not noticed it. "I guess not."

"You should drink some if you want to feel better."

"What are you doing?"

"If you're staying, I don't have clothes anywhere else," Ruga said. She trailed her hands over the dress she was wearing now. "This is not mine."

"It looks good on you," Elketh said without thinking, and slumped herself onto the bed face-first.

A warm hand pressed into Elketh's shoulders. She froze for a moment until the hand began to circle around in a soothing motion. Elketh had a short list of people who had helped her through terrible hangovers, but none of them made her feel better like this. She felt her muscles relax as the motion continued.

"You're not what I expected, either," Ruga said softly. It was not a compliment.

"I wish I could have a bath," Elketh said. "Your servant wouldn't draw me one."

Ruga snorted. "Do you not know how to draw a bath?"

"I'm a princess. I shouldn't have to," Elketh said with a groan.

"I'll get someone to do it."

"That would be much appreciated."

Too soon, the massage stopped, and Elketh's back was unbearably cold. She pushed her face farther into the soft sheets, holding back a sob. Fifty days of this. Fifty fucking days. It was forty-nine too many. How would she survive?

In a rustle of fabric, the orc princess left her. Elketh sat there for a while until she heard the door re-open, the pouring of water, the smell of the bath oils. As soon as the door closed, Elketh peeled her clammy face from the sheets and dumped herself in the scalding heat of the bath.

CHAPTER EIGHT

For a week, Ruga's life returned to normal.

After that first day when the elf princess had been sick, Elketh kept to herself, not even attending dinners. Ruga had a few discussions about it with her sister; it was better that the elf not present herself at their events at all, with the excuse of an illness from being unfamiliar with orcish food, than she show up and look like she did not want to be there.

While Astrid and her court valued a potential alliance with the elves, Ruga knew they were uneasy at Elketh's presence. She was a wild card, someone unknown to the court, and the wariness would only become worse if everyone knew the extent of the botched marriage. If Elketh could just keep her head down for the rest of the fifty days, she could return to her father, and Ruga would explain that she refused to marry someone who didn't consent. She would have to frame it like it wasn't her sister's idea but her personal preference, so as to avoid an international incident of any kind.

This seemed a very sensible idea.

In the meantime, Ruga spent her days as she always did, doing rounds of local diplomatic visits on her sister's behalf to ensure loyalty and contentment. In her free time, she wove a beautiful design into a tapestry, sat around a fire and shared stories with her friends, and took a book into her rose garden to read. She continued to sleep in the rose garden every night, although her back was complaining enough that she would likely have to make different arrangements soon. Thankfully, it hadn't rained since that first night Elketh came, and Astrid would only let Ruga bathe in the queen's suite for so long before questioning Ruga's sleeping arrangements. Ruga had made up an admirable excuse about Elketh's modesty.

For one beautiful week of normalcy, Ruga believed that she really could let the pieces of her life fall back into the places they were before the announcement of the engagement.

The first time this belief was shaken was on the eighth day after Elketh's arrival. A childhood friend of Ruga's had moved to a far away part of Torden a few years back, and Ruga finally remembered to write her a letter inquiring about her new family and inviting her to Vakker Castle for a visit. When she went to the courier house to pass off the letter, it was empty except for the clerk.

"I have a letter to post," Ruga said, squinting around at the area with suspicion creeping in. It was always notoriously busy here. They only had the most efficient people doing this important job.

The clerk wrung her hands. "I apologize, Ruga, but our couriers are all occupied."

"Occupied with what?" If there had been news of war to send out, Astrid would have notified Ruga, and Ruga would be involved in the decision-making.

"Letters," the clerk said simply, though Ruga could tell from the sheen of sweat on her forehead that it was not the full story.

A messenger ran in just then, breathing heavily, his face reddened. He blanched when he saw Ruga. "Hello."

"Hello," Ruga said. "What is keeping you so busy with letters that you can't send one of mine?"

The messenger and the clerk exchanged a look that Ruga did not like.

"We have been sending all eight messengers out every day, sometimes multiple times a day, at the behest of a...customer." Now, *that* was an unusual word. The courier service was free of charge, and the citizens of Torden were not considered "customers" by anyone except traders and shopkeepers.

"A single customer?" Ruga asked, suddenly picking up on the plurality, or lack thereof.

"Yes," the clerk said nervously.

"Well, go on. Who is it?"

The clerk slid a letter sitting on the counter over to Ruga. The envelope read: *To the Lady Morgan, Branwen.*

And Ruga could only sigh. There was only one person she knew who had any need to communicate with Branwen.

"How many letters does she send a day?" Ruga asked.

"At least thirty," the messenger said in a squeak. His horns shook a little. "We know she is your betrothed, but it is a little... Whenever we tell her we can send the letter tomorrow, she demands it be sent immediately. That they are urgent diplomatic issues and we wouldn't want to anger you."

The clerk cleared her throat. "Naturally, we questioned this, because we know you are not quick to anger. But if it was related to your ceremony plans, or some other important topic, we did not want to interfere and cause a problem."

Ruga flipped the envelope over. The seal was plain wax; if Elketh had a seal at all, her father had not given her one for her stay. She broke the seal with her fingernail and pulled out a sheet of her very own fine paper.

~~Dearest Fiddle~~ ~~Fipple~~

My love,

I am held captive here in Torden by the most inhospitable orcs you have ever seen. While my father was around, the orcs were pleasant and welcoming, and as you may have heard, I am betrothed to one of them. She is a great horned beast, unlike you. The moment he left, the orcs of Torden showed their true colors. They are quite boorish. I have sent many letters to my father for help, but he does not believe conditions are as bad as they are. Please reply at once if you are able to assist me, financially or otherwise, to get me out of here before they bring me to an early demise. I am held against my will.

Your dearest,

Elketh

A great horned beast. So that was what Elketh thought of Ruga. Clearly, the letter contained multiple lies, and Ruga found it suspicious that Elketh seemed unable to recall the recipient's name. Maybe she was getting desperate enough to contact strangers after sending so many letters.

"Has she ever received a response?" Ruga asked.

"Not one in seven days," the clerk said.

"Any letter she brings to you," Ruga said, "needs to be presented to Queen Astrid for approval first. And any that are approved may only be sent out once a day. We need our couriers for the locals, too."

"Yes, Ruga. Thank you," the clerk said, and both she and the messenger looked relieved.

That was the end of that. Ruga would tell Astrid to keep the letters where she could screen them.

The next day, Ruga had ten letters to sift through, but the day after that, there were only three, and the next day, none at all. Elketh was surprisingly astute. She either realized her letters were not being delivered, or she knew they were being read and wanted them private. Ruga hadn't noticed Elketh leaving her room to go to the courier house, but at least there were no other complaints.

The day after the letters stopped, there was another incident. Elketh had been quietly accepting meals in her room. Ruga frequently interrogated the kitchen staff who brought food to her.

None of them liked to do it, but all of them claimed that while Elketh never said "thank you" or showed any other general courtesies that should be given to someone providing a service, she also never demanded extra of them. Until, at breakfast, the kitchen boy came crying back, still carrying the food tray, trailing spilled porridge behind him down the stairs.

"What is it?" Ruga asked. The boy was an orc of maybe sixty years, still very young and sensitive. Ruga had to get up from her own meal to help him, earning a stern look from Astrid.

"She said she won't eat anything until someone ferries her home. She was yelling and throwing things and—" The boy dissolved into sobs.

Ruga felt a headache coming on. She didn't want to know what her rooms looked like or what possessions of hers had been destroyed.

"Princess Elketh," she called at the door. How absurd, to be a stranger in her own bedchamber. "Princess Elketh?"

There was a crashing noise. Two guards from each end of the hall charged to Ruga's side.

"Please do not destroy my things. Can we talk?"

Another big crash, and then silence. Without expecting much, Ruga tried the doorknob. Locked.

"I have a key, and I'm coming in. I'm going to count to five."

The door swung open. Elketh stood there, chest heaving, her eyes bloodshot and her hair askew. She was wearing an indecent amount of clothing, just a shift with one short sleeve so far down her shoulder, it exposed the top half of her breast. Ruga politely averted her eyes.

"What do *you* want?" Elketh asked with venom. Her breath smelled of mead. Even in the disarray, Ruga felt the anger in the elf's shaking body.

It seemed unfair that someone so beautiful could have such a rotten personality.

"I need you to stop harassing my kitchen staff, which I already warned you about once," Ruga said, maintaining her composure. "And I don't want to stop you from sending letters, or drinking, or any of your other vices, but if you abuse any of these privileges, we will take them away like the captors you think we are."

"I am on hunger strike," Elketh announced.

"Hunger strike but not drink strike, I see," Ruga retorted. She pushed into the antechamber past Elketh; the elf stumbled backwards and Ruga caught her wrist, then smoothly flicked the shift's sleeve back in place.

"I need better clothes," Elketh said. Her shift was indeed stained with yellow circles around the armpits, and splotches of spilled violet, aging brown. "I only had the one dress and yours don't fit me."

Ruga turned to her wardrobe, hissing unexpectedly at the sight. The door was ajar and half her dresses littered the floor, some of them only trampled and others nearly torn in half.

She had sourced fabric and sewn most of those dresses. Clothes could be replaced, Ruga had to remind herself. Elketh was in a difficult position and she wasn't the type of person to let her hardships go unnoticed. She needed compassion, not punishment.

"We can get you clothes," Ruga said, "if you'll come with me to the tailor and have your measurements taken. And we can accommodate diet changes if you do not like our fare."

"I want a servant," Elketh spat. She leaned heavily against the wall at Ruga's bedside. Ruga tried not to wince at the sight of a book ripped to shreds around the bed, the debris scattered in a wide radius of torn pages. "Someone to draw my baths and do my hair and send my letters."

"Only the queen has a lady's maid," Ruga said calmly, aware of the two guards still waiting in the doorway. If she hoped that Elketh's discontent with her accommodations would remain secret, she could surely let those hopes go. "You made it impossible for Torden's citizenry to send letters. I implore you not to clog up the system."

Elketh's mouth opened and closed. She rubbed at her eye. "Okay. I won't send any letters."

Well, Ruga thought. She wasn't completely unreasonable. "If you can do tasks a servant would do yourself, we encourage you to."

Whatever guilt Elketh initially appeared to feel at understanding her level of inconvenience dissipated. "Find someone to draw me a bath. I need one. Now. And have them bring me some garments closer to my size."

Every time Ruga offered a solution, it only provoked Elketh, like she wanted a target for her anger and wouldn't be satisfied until she had one. So that was how it was going to be.

"No," Ruga said, and left the room. She nodded a silent thanks to the guards, unable to speak lest she express the frustration she was bottling up, and she found the elf librarian, similar in stature to Elketh, and asked if she had any dresses Ruga could buy off of her, because she did not trust Elketh not to destroy them.

Elketh's goal was obvious: she wanted to be so belligerent that Astrid sent her home. If Ruga had her way, Astrid would never hear a word of exactly how difficult Elketh was acting. It would do both Elketh and the entire country of Torden a favor that Elketh not be sent home in disgrace. Ruga did not want to think how the elf king would react to his daughter being forcibly returned, if he was the kind of person who pulled the wool over her eyes to force her into a marriage she had no interest in.

She returned to her bedchamber. The door was still ajar, and the princess was rifling through the wardrobe, muttering to herself. Quietly and calmly, Ruga shifted half-ripped pages off of the bed and pulled the sheets taut, and then set the dress on top of them.

Then, she went into the bathroom, drew the bath Elketh so badly wanted, and left before the elf could see her.

CHAPTER NINE

Getting out of this situation was going to be much harder than Elketh thought.

If the conditions themselves made Elketh angry, the orc princess with her unyielding patience only infuriated Elketh more. Elketh yearned to see Ruga crack, to watch her yell and throw things like she felt something, too. Elketh did not like to be the only one frustrated with the world. Other people had to share her misery, and if they didn't, she would make them.

At least Ruga had found someone to draw her baths. Elketh eased herself into the steaming water of the giant floor tub, probing several bruises she didn't remember getting. She had to hatch a plan, and soon, to get out of here.

Nothing was working.

No one responded to her letters—not her mother and not her brother and none, even, of her favorite lovers.

She considered her options. Waiting thirty-eight days and then explaining that she wouldn't give in to her father was out of the question. Whatever Ruga's problem was, at least she didn't condone the unwilling betrothal. The only thing Elketh could think to do was offend the orcs so badly, they forcibly sent her away. Then her father would have no choice but to accept her back into his good graces.

And Elketh was sure he wasn't all that serious about disinheriting her. Put in her position, he surely would not have married someone outside of their home islands.

Dinner that night was sent up to her rooms, as it always was, but this time, someone in the kitchens had been careful to only include dishes Elketh would have eaten on her island. The gesture should have been thoughtful, but swallowing down the sweet flavors just made her more irritable. She went to bed that night plotting something so egregious that she would be sent off. Exile would be preferable, so her father couldn't send her right back.

Maybe she could cause a diplomatic incident.

Her dreams were fearful, flitting things about corridors that ended in traps.

Elketh woke to the sun in her face and a barrage of knocks on the door. The kitchen staff had given up on being so insistent with her; it had to be someone important.

She got out of bed, flattening her hair, and then donned the simple dress the orc had left her yesterday before anyone could see her in the state of disarray she'd allowed herself to fall into.

When Elketh abandoned this place, she had an image of herself the way she wanted her father to see her: formidable, dangerous, unstoppable, defiant. The skalds back on Branwen would sing of her bravery in defying the wyrd given to her.

The thought of being the center of attention for millennia to come cheered Elketh up so much, she was actually smiling when Ruga opened the door.

The orc was visibly surprised by the mood shift. "I told you I would take you to the tailor today," she said.

"Good morning to you, too," Elketh said, chipper.

Ruga looked Elketh up and down. "Well. We better be off."

Elketh followed her into the hallway, her stomach growling. Someone had left a tray of food outside her door. Elketh bent to pick it up, disgruntled. "Revolting that your servants would leave good food on the floor."

"Once more, they are not servants, just regular kitchen staff. And I told them that they didn't have to interact with you if they didn't want to. I think that's only fair, considering how you treated them."

Elketh stared blankly at Ruga, her mouth full of buttered bread. "I am not that difficult," she said, knowing full well she had been as inconvenient as she could to everyone around her.

"If you say so," Ruga said with a thin little smile that made Elketh want to rip those tusks off.

On their way out, the orc stopped at the library and chatted with its librarian, an elf. Elketh gawked at her with interest. They didn't have orcs working in Branwen; Olwen had an orc, a blacksmith named Gerta, but she was unique to the Elven Islands, and Elketh had never met her. It was odd to see an elf working in an orc place, but then, the orcs had humans running around, too.

"Hello," Elketh said to the elf librarian, pleasantly, when Ruga went off to find a book.

"Hi," the librarian said, as though she did not want to be there at all. She pushed her glasses up her face so as to peer better down her nose at Elketh.

"So," Elketh said to fill the silence, "an elf in orc country, eh?"

The librarian rolled her eyes at Elketh. "Aren't you also an elf in orc country?"

Elketh simmered with rage but covered it with a smile. If Elketh played her cards right, and she had as much in common with the librarian as she hoped, she could get laid later.

"Well, you know why I'm here. How did you end up working at the library?"

"Oh, you know," the librarian said. "Got myself caught up in the human wars. Then ended up in Lynby's war, and now I'm hoping to get myself involved in this one."

Elketh balked. The human wars were up north, though Elketh couldn't picture their place on a map. Borders that shifted so often they weren't worth writing down, never-ending battles between human warlords. All Elketh knew about the wars were from merchants who passed through Branwen. Exactly how an elf librarian ended up in a human war and then an orc war defied Elketh's (admittedly small) knowledge of the world. The librarian must've been lying.

Clearly enjoying herself, the librarian threw back her head and laughed at Elketh's expense. Elketh cleared her throat, cheeks warming. The librarian liked to play, and Elketh liked to play, too. This conversation wasn't unsalvageable.

"I've never been in here before," she said, running a finger over the edge of an ancient book spine. It came away dustless.

"You don't say." The librarian began to turn away from her.

"Would you give me a tour?" Elketh leaned on the counter, tugging down on her dress with one hand to reveal her cleavage. "I'd love to see the place."

The librarian turned back to her, glanced once down her dress, and said, "Sure."

Elketh hurried to follow the librarian around the corner. Maybe she could get laid *today*.

"You may have these back on your island," the librarian said, gesturing broadly.

"Have what?" Elketh asked.

"Books."

Elketh's eye started to twitch and didn't stop until the "tour" was over. It consisted entirely of the librarian pointing to different spines and saying, as though she had something new to present each time, "And these are...books," "Finally, we've arrived at books," and, with aplomb, "This is a book."

Hidden around a corner was a mystical case with a lantern flicking over it. Elketh spotted a glint of gold out of the corner of her eye as the librarian hurried her away. "Wait, what's that?" she asked, and quickly added, "If you say books, I'm going to stab you in the eye."

"It's the ceremonial crown," the librarian said with an exaggerated sigh. "Keep your greasy fingers off the glass."

Ruga was waiting at the counter when they came back.

"What a lovely tour that was," Elketh said, encroaching on the librarian's space and trying to take her hand.

"Your breath smells awful," was all the librarian said, before cataloguing Ruga's selection and moving on with her life, ignoring Elketh as though she wasn't there.

"Your librarian is mean." Elketh breathed subtly into her cupped hand and inhaled through her nose. It wasn't like anyone had given her time for personal hygiene that morning. "And uninformative."

"I think you have an off-putting presence."

"I'm well-liked back in Branwen," Elketh said, fuming.

Ruga handed the book off to one of the guards as she passed—apparently, it was to go to the queen. Interesting. Did the queen not have time to get books herself? More importantly, why was Torden so willing to give up its princess if she ran so many favors for the queen? Surely, she was important enough to keep around. Unless a lot was riding on the marriage alliance.

An uncomfortable pit formed in Elketh's stomach.

"We're really going to the tailor? To get me new dresses?" she said.

"Yes. I keep my promises, although you may not think so."

They reached the castle gates and were let out by two guards who exchanged pleasantries with Ruga. Elketh wondered, as she found herself doing more and more, if the close relationship between royals and guards was a Torden custom or a Ruga thing. Elketh had hardly said a word to one of her father's guards her whole life.

Ruga led Elketh down a busy street of peddlers. Elketh had to cover her nose as they got closer to the harbor; the fishmongers mongered their smelly wares everywhere she looked. It was a familiar, almost comfortingly repulsive smell. Elketh did not like to spend time with the fishmongers on her island, but they shared waters with these orcs, and thus shared the same kinds of fish. They were much better-smelling roasted on a spit than they were raw at the market. She inhaled a deep breath of fresh air as they turned the corner onto a street of little shops.

A bell rang as Ruga entered a shop labeled *seamstress* with ruffly dresses out front. Elketh wasn't big on ruffles. She preferred dresses that allowed for mobility, like for a great escape. Hopefully the seamstress had more she could make.

Elketh trailed behind Ruga into the shop and found Ruga hugging someone. A squat old orc with wrinkles sagging down their face.

"Ruga," the seamstress said fondly. "I didn't know if I would see you again."

"I missed you too." Ruga ran her hands over several swathes of multicolored fabric. "Wow, you got a new shipment. These are lovely."

Elketh cleared her throat.

"Ah, Dag, this is Elketh. She's..." Ruga swallowed. "She's in need of a dress or two."

"Make it two," Elketh said, smiling charmingly at the seamstress. Dag. A name like someone being stabbed. Ideally that did not apply to the seamstress's needlework. "I am ready. Take my measurements."

The seamstress approached her. Elketh realized that taking her measurements would mean the seamstress touching her with their crotchety old fingers. Dag chuckled to themself, clucking a mouth of missing teeth. "You've got yourself a beauty, Ruga."

"Ah...thanks," Ruga said, shifting uncomfortably.

They did not know that the marriage wasn't going to happen.

Elketh narrowed her eyes at Ruga. This conversation did not work in favor of Torden following through on letting Elketh out of the arrangement.

"It was nice to have you around the shop," the seamstress said, circling Elketh in a way that made her hunch her shoulders. "My hands are getting too old for some things."

"Dag is nearly a millennium old," Ruga informed Elketh.

"Lovely," Elketh said, flatly. "Do you make dresses, too...dear?"

"Ruga makes wonderful dresses. She made the one she's wearing now," the seamstress said. They were rummaging around in a drawer.

The dress Ruga wore was quite nice, a simple, deep purple number accentuated with a leather belt. The color matched her hair. It fit somewhat loosely, but her muscles bulged through it, which was the only thing Elketh really cared about when it came to assessing raiments.

"How lucky am I," Elketh said, saccharine, "that my own bride-to-be can take my measurements for me."

It was too hard to resist. Elketh could avoid being felt up by the old orc, and she could annoy Ruga to boot. Ruga took the bait without complaint, helping Dag extract the measuring tape from the drawer.

Elketh held out her arms.

"Are you going to strip?" Ruga asked. "I can hardly measure your inseam when you're in a dress. Haven't you been to a tailor before?"

Elketh was sure her measurements hadn't changed in over a hundred years. "Not recently," she admitted. "You don't need an inseam measurement for dresses."

"Do you ever wear trousers?"

"Sometimes."

"Strip, please."

The seamstress pulled a curtain away from the wall for privacy. Elketh stepped behind it and fumbled with the back of her dress until it was in a pile on the floor, leaving her in just her smallclothes: the band covering her breasts and the wrapped cloth covering her ass.

Ruga came at her with the measuring tape. Elketh stiffened as Ruga's hand brushed her skin, but Ruga was clinical with her touch, a professional, and her fingers were surprisingly warm against the goosebumps on Elketh's skin. Elketh stood still as Ruga ran the measuring tape against her spine, around her neck, down her arms and the outside of her leg. Ruga called out numbers as she did so. The scratching of nib on paper was audible from the other side of the curtain.

"You should've been a court jester instead of a princess," Ruga said, keeping her eyes only on the numbers of the measuring tape. "Do you really need *me* to take your measurements? Don't you know any of them?"

"I just ask for more dresses, and they're delivered to me," Elketh said. The touching was making her cheeks a bit flushed, especially when Ruga held the tape around her waist. "I didn't want that wrinkly orc to touch me."

"That's rude. Dag is very kind," Ruga said.

Elketh stumbled a bit when Ruga ran the tape around her hips. Instinctively, Ruga grabbed the back of Elketh's thigh to steady her, then quickly let go. She called out a number, unfazed.

Elketh was somewhat fazed.

"This marriage thing," Elketh said, and then couldn't make herself continue.

Ruga gestured for Elketh to lift her arms and measured her bust against the strophium. "I told you, I won't let it happen. If you could just keep that to yourself for now, though, we can figure out how we want to disseminate that information to the people."

"It's quite important, isn't it?" Elketh whispered. She was conscious of Ruga's closeness to her face and the librarian's comment about her breath. "For your people."

"Of course it is," Ruga said. "This isn't something we do every day. There was a lot of hope riding on it." She called out another number after wrapping the tape around Elketh's arm. "I'm going to measure your inseam now, all right?"

"All right," Elketh said. She held the top as Ruga ran the tape down the inside of Elketh's leg, which only made her more flushed. The knot in her stomach was getting worse, the more she talked to Ruga about the marriage. If only her father had given her time to prepare for this, maybe... Well, no. She wouldn't want to do it no matter what. But it did not seem particularly fair to the orcs that her father had offered them someone who didn't want to be there.

"Ruga, you are inseaming-ly helpful today," Dag said, and Elketh flinched at the corniness even as Ruga barked a rough laugh. Dag exchanged many an inside joke with Ruga, the context of which Elketh could only guess at. Their banter was so natural. It was readily apparent that Ruga had been coming here for years to help with dresses, and that the two were close friends.

"You're quite the extrovert," Elketh said.

"I wouldn't call myself one," Ruga said to her. Elketh liked that Ruga used a quieter voice to talk to her than to Dag, like their conversation was worth keeping private.

"You have many friends."

"I like solitude more than I like being around others," Ruga said. She completed her last measurement and stood, rolling her shoulder.

"Even the librarian seemed to like you. The only thing she liked about me was my body. She kept checking me out." Elketh didn't know what prompted her to keep up the conversation, only that maybe *she* was extroverted and needed the social interaction, even if it came from a stranger. She didn't believe Ruga was a secret introvert, either.

"I think she was looking at your dress," Ruga said, "because I purchased it from her and gifted it to you. It suits her better."

She winked, and left Elketh behind the curtain to scrabble with the dress.

Elketh's blood boiled.

She came out to find Ruga and Dag speaking in hushed voices. They became quiet when they saw her. Elketh was sure they had been talking about her, maybe making fun of her, even.

She stormed out of the shop and back to the castle.

CHAPTER TEN

A couple days later, Ruga watched the delivery of clothes come in. Dag had help from those in the community to make them, to Ruga's discomfort, because they were passionate about the alliance and wanted to help. The shop's apprentice brought the clothes with enthusiastic tales of Torden's citizenry sewing overnight to assist the seamstress, teams of people working together in a system where the dresses came together in mere hours.

Ruga had the clothes delivered directly to Elketh rather than taking them to her. At least that would get the elf off her back. She had a sneaking suspicion based on Elketh's personality alone that the elf princess wasn't going to make it easy to live through the remaining thirty-five days.

Elketh confused her, Ruga had to admit. She couldn't tell if Elketh was obtuse or just hadn't thought through what the marriage alliance meant to Torden. Why would Elketh ask Ruga if the marriage was important? Did she think the orcs just invited anybody to marry someone in a highly respected position for fun?

Ruga snipped the next rose stem a little too hard at the wrong angle. She wiped her forehead with the back of her hand. This was supposed to be a calming activity, cultivating the roses to her pleasure, working up a sweat in the summer heat. It was hard to do while distracted.

Distractions were all she had.

In Ruga's nightmares, Elketh jumped into the water repeatedly. Now, she thought of the conversation Dag had pulled her aside for.

We've been worried that you wouldn't have enough in common with an elf from the Islands, Dag had said. *It's obvious that you two have chemistry. I can't wait to share the good news with everyone.*

Not only was the assessment wrong, but it would have damaging effects when Torden's citizenry found out the truth. Logically, Ruga knew that the people, especially those who lived close to the capital of Vakker, were loyal and loving to Queen Astrid. There was an ugly seed of doubt that took root in her, however, that when the marriage negotiations officially fell through, some would revolt. To Branwen's king, she might have to pretend it was her decision, something that would hurt Torden and Branwen's relationship as trading partners. To Torden's people, she had to make it look like Elketh's fault, but not in a way that would have people carting pitchforks to King Gareth's castle.

It was a delicate balance. Thinking about it made Ruga warm separately from the heat.

She nearly sliced an entire finger off when someone stepped up behind her.

"These are gorgeous. You garden?"

The elf princess, in the flesh.

Ruga calmed her unsteady heart. "Yes, this is my rose garden. Haven't you seen it from my window?"

To Dag's credit, the elf was stunning. In spite of Elketh's protests about having her inseam measured, she wore trousers now, with a pair of sharp leather boots that crept past her knee. Her loose tunic looked comfortable in the steadily climbing heat of this early summer day, carrying the breeze with it.

She gave off the impression of a rogue hero out of a skald's tale. "I suppose I saw it when I ran away. I don't like to look out the window much. Too sunny."

Too sunny? Ruga liked the sun, liked that it woke her up early so she could get a head start on the day. It mildly offended her that the elf was sleeping in her rooms without appreciating their amenities. "I like where the window is because I can see the garden up there whenever I like."

"Perhaps you should have put your garden on another side of the castle," Elketh said, leaning in to smell a rose. Her long, midnight-black hair was shiny in the sun—she'd either done something to condition it or convinced someone who wasn't supposed to be doing servant-like tasks to help her out. Ruga got a whiff of her hair oil, a pleasant floral smell.

"The roses catch the early morning sun if they're on the east side. They could die without it."

"I hadn't considered that." Elketh stepped on one of the rose heads Ruga had clipped and then covered her mouth. "Oh, were you saving that? Why are you cutting them?"

"I was going to give them to... It doesn't matter. I'm getting rid of the dead heads. So they can grow better." Ruga regained her senses and found another stem that needed work. "Do you garden much?"

"No, not at all."

Ruga watched the way Elketh ran her hand over the roses like they were precious. How strange to see her doing something so normal after her reign of terror. Curiosity got the best of Ruga. "What are you doing out here?"

"Exploring. I didn't expect to run into you. Is this one of those things you like to do alone?"

Ruga nodded.

"Can you show me what you're doing with the roses?"

The sudden interest roused Ruga's suspicion. "Er, not to be rude, but...I was under the impression that you didn't like me."

Elketh straightened her posture, brushing some of her waist-length hair over her shoulder. "I'm undecided on that. I'm also very bored up there in the castle. None of your people will talk to me."

Ruga tried not to stare. Either Elketh had no idea her behavior was undesirable to the castle inhabitants, many of whom knew firsthand of her antics, if not her reluctance, or she just didn't care. "Sure, I'll show you." Ruga tugged on a stem, running her finger down the leaves, explaining how she chose which ones to deadhead and which to leave alone, where she wanted the roses to flourish and where she wanted to curb their growth.

"It's more complicated than I would have thought," Elketh said. In the end, she refused the clippers. "I'm scared of messing up."

Did she really care so much about Ruga's garden? "That's thoughtful. But not necessarily a cure for your boredom."

"I learned something, at least," Elketh said, rocking on her heels. She was grinning. Ruga was scared to call attention to the good mood, lest the princess change her mind and go back to jumping in harbors or getting sloppily drunk in public.

"Is there anything you like to do?" Ruga asked, feeling a little indulgent because the elf had been so patient listening to her. "How do you fill your time back home?"

"Elaborate games," Elketh said, waving her hand in a way that made it seem like they would be too complicated for Ruga's simple mind to understand. "Swimming. Food and drink. Pestering my brother. Archery."

"We have an archery range," Ruga said, "at the soldiers' training grounds."

Elketh's face lit up. "Really?"

"I'll show you," Ruga said, hoping she wouldn't regret it.

The archery range was busy when they arrived. Guards stood shoulder-to-shoulder with orcish children. Ruga recognized one of the orcs, a pastry baker, as a guard helped him adjust his form. The field was open and lush with grass, filled with the chirping of birds and the thwacking of arrows hitting targets.

Ruga led Elketh to the bow racks. "You can pick out which one you like," she said, and waited, curious.

It became immediately apparent that Elketh *did* know what she was doing when it came to archery; she passed over the smaller training bows and went into picking up different kinds, holding them close to her face as though examining the quality of the wood. Her fingers twitched with excitement.

This was, perhaps, the first time Ruga ever saw her genuinely happy. In spite of Ruga's reservations, the feeling was contagious. If she'd known the archery range would make Elketh so comfortable, she would have brought her here several weeks ago.

"There are a lot of random people here," Elketh said, selecting one that was simple-looking to Ruga's untrained eye. "Are you so desperate for soldiers?"

Elketh knew so little of orc customs. "No, that's not how we do things," Ruga said. "We have such long lives." As did elves, but it felt like an insult to point out they weren't using their time well. "It would be a waste not to explore different interests until we find the things we love."

Elketh looked at the training grounds anew, taking in each of the outliers with revelation. "Do you have hobbies other than gardening?" she asked. "Wait, don't answer. Dressmaking?"

Just two skills? "Among some others."

"Does that mean you tried out archery?" Elketh asked.

"Yes," Ruga said, tugging at the collar of her dress. "I have to admit, it's not for me."

Elketh nodded, a bit dazed. "Where can I shoot?"

"Here." Ruga brought her to an area that was better secluded. "Ah, any of the targets. Or the trees." The trees were marked up, but the targets were fresh, replenished whenever they got too worn-down, some of them big and low and some of them small and at varying heights.

Inexplicably, she was nervous. Maybe it was because watching Elketh do one of her favorite things in the world seemed a violation of her privacy.

"Every elf should know how to hunt in case of emergency. You never know when a rabbit can save your life."

Ruga blanched. "Please don't shoot rabbits, if any happen to come on the range. I don't know if I could handle it."

"Not big on rabbits?" Elketh asked, running fingers over the arch of the bow.

"I don't eat meat."

At this, Elketh gave a startled laugh, as though she couldn't imagine it. "Why?"

"Is it so bad to not want to eat animals?"

Elketh snorted, lifting an arrow from the barrel set at their station. "You really are a gentle soul, aren't you?"

The comment left Ruga flustered. She stepped back to give Elketh space as she notched the arrow. The bow was nearly as tall as she was, with a simple curve. The name came to Ruga from a far-off memory: longbow. Astrid liked archery, unlike her, but then Astrid seemed to be good at everything, which was why Torden elected her as queen.

Ruga stood mesmerized as Elketh pulled the string back, her body relaxed effortlessly, practically made for this specific activity. A muscle bulged on her arm when she brought the fletching of the arrow almost to her mouth. Elketh released the arrow directly into the center of a target and let out a satisfied sigh.

"Impressive," Ruga said, which was a bit of an understatement.

"How many can I do?"

"As many as you like."

And she did. Ruga couldn't help but watch every time as Elketh nocked arrows and loosed them into the various targets. She noticed things she didn't expect to, like that Elketh only gripped the long part of the arrow with two fingers, lining the arrow along her forefinger as she set it up. She noticed that Elketh bit her lip every time, right before the arrow sailed, and she noticed especially that muscle every time it bulged.

It would have been easy to find an excuse to leave Elketh there by herself. Thinking of the other things Ruga could do—go around town and check on people, run errands for her sister—seemed too socially demanding, though, and this was fun, hiding in the shade of the trees with an almost-stranger. While Elketh was more of an irritant than anything, Ruga couldn't help but notice she was interesting, too, maybe the most interesting thing to happen to her in a while.

They'd been there for over an hour when Elketh's skin began to gleam with perspiration. She proffered the bow to Ruga. "Do you want to give it a try?" she asked.

"I don't know if that's a good idea," Ruga said. "Someone might lose an eye."

"I can help you," Elketh said.

How could this be the same elf who risked her life to run away from Ruga? As if in a trance, Ruga took the bow from Elketh, holding it stiffly.

"Lift it higher," Elketh instructed.

It tired Ruga's arm to do so. She tried anyway, lifting it up, shaking a bit with the effort. Or maybe from the weight of the dark pair of eyes on her. "Like this?"

"Indeed. Only—lower your shoulder a bit. No, not like that. Can I—?" Elketh had come very close, reaching a tentative hand to Ruga's shoulder. Ruga swallowed and nodded. Elketh nudged Ruga's shoulder down with one hand, raising her forearm with the other. "Relaxed, but straight."

Elketh smelled faintly of sweat, a tad earthy, with that floral overtone of her hair oil. Ruga held the bow with two fingers like she'd seen Elketh do and nocked the arrow along her forefinger.

"Good, you were paying attention," Elketh said, her breath caressing Ruga's ear.

Loudly, Ruga swallowed again. She dragged the fletching and the string back to her mouth, feeling the same muscle she saw on Elketh's forearm twinge. "Can I let it go yet?" If she ever knew them, she was blanking on the proper archery terms. In fact, her whole mind was blank as a painter's canvas.

"Not yet. Your other arm isn't...here." Elketh's hand wrapped around the bottom of Ruga's elbow where she had it bent by her face and gently lifted it up.

She didn't release her grip.

"Now," she breathed.

Ruga let the arrow loose. She had no idea where it landed, only that it didn't make the firm noise of Elketh's arrows. She was too busy thinking of Elketh at the seamstress, in just her smallclothes, and how this felt strangely more intimate than that. Together, the images that came to mind, unbidden, of Elketh's smooth, bare skin, of her toned torso, and their closeness now—it was all too much.

"That wasn't half bad," Elketh said, just a few inches from Ruga. As if only noticing now that they were still touching, she dropped her hand and stepped back.

Ruga tried not to look at Elketh, to give herself time to gather her thoughts.

"Do you want to try again?" Elketh asked. She already had another arrow rolling around in her hands.

"I...um. All right."

Elketh handed her the arrow. Their fingers brushed against each other as Ruga took it. "I used to pick up women like this," Elketh said.

"What?"

"It was a good excuse for a lot of touching," she said, and then shrugged like it meant nothing. "I have to confess that while I'm good at archery, I'm not a very good teacher."

Ruga set the arrow into place with the knowledge she had from watching Elketh's form. She kept her shoulder low instead of letting it ride up, and then raised her other elbow so it was aligned with her arm nearest Elketh and the arrow. Elketh might not be a good teacher, but Ruga was an adept student. "Were you flirting with me?" Ruga asked finally, the bow taut. Her gaze was carefully focused on the center of the target, though she didn't know if looking right at it would help.

Elketh didn't respond. Ruga loosed the arrow and it landed on the target this time, halfway between the center and the edge, with a loud, satisfying noise.

Her knuckle stung a little where it had kicked back against the wood. She focused on that until the silence became unbearable, and then she gave in and looked at Elketh, who smirked as she took the longbow back from Ruga, careful not to let their hands touch this time.

Ruga looked at Elketh, and she couldn't stop looking.

CHAPTER ELEVEN

If there was one thing Elketh hadn't expected during her stay in Torden, it was experiencing the power trip she got from teasing an attractive woman into getting flustered. The archery lesson—if you could call it that, though to her credit, Ruga did learn something—had fulfilled one of Elketh's favorite indulgences. She considered that she must be some level of desperate to be seriously considering Ruga in that way. It had been a few weeks since she'd had sex, she reminded herself. She was just horny. It didn't mean anything.

It wouldn't do to get chummy with someone she fully planned to screw over, anyway. The only downside of her plan was that she sort of liked Ruga. She liked spending time with her earlier that day, whatever their previous experiences. Elketh had seldom come across someone who seemed so honest and open.

No matter how Elketh felt about the orc, she was initiating the real first phase of her plan to get evicted from Torden for good. It involved the elf librarian, who hadn't even given Elketh her name, and if Elketh played her cards right, she could kill two birds with one stone.

"So," Elketh said, to get the attention of the librarian, who seemed to have little interest in anything but her book.

The librarian grunted in response and didn't look up. Elketh cleared her throat, leaning over the counter like she had before, only she'd made sure to wear one of her new dresses now. She had to practically spill her breasts out into the book before the librarian paid attention to her.

"Is there something I can help you with?" the librarian asked.

"I missed your name before. I would love to have it," Elketh said, blasting her full charm.

"I don't think that's necessary." The librarian turned back to her book, tugging it away from where Elketh had pinned it under her chest.

Damn. So it was going to be like that. "What are you reading?" Elketh asked.

"Nothing you're smart enough to understand."

Unlike Ruga, Elketh's patience only went so far. "I thought it would be nice to bond with someone like myself. I don't understand why you're not interested."

"I've been around orcs so long, it doesn't matter to me whether some elf comes in with a sour attitude and tries to befriend me. I'm comfortable with the friends I have," the librarian said, but she slid a string into the book to mark her place and closed it.

"What about dating them?" Transparently, Elketh was thinking of Ruga, of the way the orc had reacted when Elketh touched her. "Have you been with any orcs?"

"Of course," the librarian snapped. "Are you here to talk about my sexual history, or did you have something you actually wanted from the library?"

"I could be part of yours."

"My what?"

"Your sexual history."

The librarian snorted. "I don't think you could handle me, honey."

"So you have a thing just for orcs, then? Or maybe men?"

She looked Elketh up and down before responding. "Let's say my thing is *not you.*"

"What's it like to have sex with an orc?"

The librarian pushed her spectacles up her nose. "Getting a little personal, are we?"

"I'm just trying to see the benefits."

"You're insinuating that haven't warmed Ruga's bed yet."

Elketh coughed to cover the fact that she'd completely forgotten she was supposed to pretend everything was all right with the arrangement. It wouldn't matter soon, anyway, she reassured herself. "We're waiting until marriage."

"Waiting until marriage with Ruga, but ready to go with me."

Elketh smiled, all teeth. "Perhaps."

"They have tongues." The librarian made a gesture with her hand poking out of her mouth that Elketh did not understand. "Penetrative tongues."

"Who?"

"Orcs. Didn't you want to know what the sex was like? It's good."

It was Elketh's turn to burn with embarrassment. Like during the extremely uninformative tour, the librarian was trying her best to make Elketh feel unwelcome by making her discomfited.

"Is this conversation over?" the librarian asked. She glanced behind her at a clock on the wall. "I'm not giving you what you want."

"I was really here for a quiet place to read," Elketh said, defensively, even though it was a lie.

"*Really*," the librarian said.

"Yes."

"Well, I showed you around last time. Go ahead."

Elketh kept her smile all the way around the corner until she was completely out of sight. The great benefit to being perceived as annoying was that she'd basically guaranteed the librarian wouldn't follow her.

She headed right for the ceremonial crown behind its glass. Where she thought she'd be able to pry the glass with her fingers or a thin piece of metal she could use as a lockpick, it was actually latched with some kind of binding agent. With an arrow from her bag, Elketh painstakingly chipped away at the adhesive with the pointed tip. The glue worried her. If this crown was brought out so seldom that they glued it into an unopenable case, it wasn't likely to be noticed missing.

This was just the first attempt of potentially many to get herself sent home. The thought wasn't as reassuring as she liked. She couldn't jump ahead. Her arm was tired by the time the case began to wiggle open, but sure enough, she soon held the crown in her hands, its old gold in dire need of a polish. She lowered the glass back down, the gluey bits sticking enough that it wasn't immediately noticeable it'd been broken into.

Hopefully, someone would think it was supposed to be taken out for some reason or another by someone who wasn't Elketh.

The crown went into her bag in case the librarian noticed her holding it. As she left, the librarian didn't acknowledge her existence.

Elketh made a beeline for the kitchens.

They were bustling with activity as the servants—*kitchen staff*, Ruga would correct her—prepared dinner for the orcs. Unlike in the library, Elketh had a lot of attention here. She would definitely be remembered.

The perfect excuse came to her: she would have to play up how difficult she was. And that meant complaining.

"The food made here," she announced to the entirety of the kitchens, making most of them stop to stare, "is so abysmal that I can hardly eat it."

Satisfyingly, the head chef's hulking face began to turn an impressive shade of purple. Elketh stopped to pick up a slimy fish and lifted it to her nose as she held her breath.

"How old are these fish? Were they caught several weeks ago? They're *rancid*," she said, and the human preparing the fish clenched his knife tighter.

She took another moment to berate someone about the meals sent to her room, garnering several eye rolls, and then pretended to carry her tantrum into the cellar with a final insult, swiping a meat tenderizer as she went.

"I should have come down here a long time ago," she said to herself as she passed walls with bottles of mead packed side-by-side. She set the old crown carefully on the floor. It really was a dingy little thing. Hardly worth calling a national heirloom. She hoped people missed it enough.

Elketh gave the crown a few light pats with the meat tenderizer. It wasn't particularly thick gold, if it was gold at all, she supposed so that it wasn't too heavy to wear. This crown had a layer of fabric along the inside, whereas the one the real orc queen wore was simpler, silver and small without all this extra adorning.

Toward the pointed tips, the crown was delicate as lacework. The tips bent with even gentle taps of the tenderizer.

An image of Ruga's face at the archery range flashed through Elketh's mind. She hesitated. They wouldn't have any more bonding moments after she followed through with this plan. And Ruga had been so kind.

"I'm sorry," Elketh said aloud. "This has to be done."

Elketh raised the tenderizer above her head with both hands and slammed it down on the crown. And then she did it again, and again, until it had cracked and bent, until little pieces chipped off and flew in every direction. Her arms bounced against the crown until they grew sore, but it was a great outlet for her rage.

The cellar door banged open. Elketh stopped, her ears and arms ringing so much that she barely noticed the figure who came down until they'd dragged her up by one of her long ears. She yelped, stumbling after the person as they shoved her out of the room, past the staff, who all gawked at her in surprise. It took her nearly a minute to realize that the person was the librarian and that she was unfathomably furious.

The librarian pushed her up a set of stairs, kicking the backs of her shins when she slowed down too much. "Where are we going?" Elketh gasped, her ear still pinched between the librarian's fingers.

A muscle worked in the librarian's jaw. She didn't answer. Elketh struggled to keep up with the librarian—whenever she fell behind, it hurt more. They passed a trio of guards in the middle of a long hallway. One of them took an immediate interest in the commotion.

"Vera?" the guard called, and when the librarian didn't answer, she followed, a surge of footsteps that Elketh could hear but not see. "Vera!"

Numbly, Elketh registered that the librarian's name was Vera. She didn't like that name much, either.

"Vera! What do you think you're doing?"

The guard's hand clamped over Vera's arm. Vera released Elketh, who rubbed her ear, moaning in slight exaggeration. This hall was peculiar compared to the one where she stayed. There was an elaborate door at the end of it and only one other door about halfway down, which the guards had been leaning out of. She didn't understand where all the space went.

"She *ruined* the ceremonial crown," Vera spat. "She smashed it with a hammer."

"How was she able to get past you?" the guard demanded. "You're supposed to be watching it."

Vera threw the guard off of her. "Mind your fucking business, Hedda. I have to take her to the queen." Her eyes narrowed on Elketh. "I hope they behead you for this."

Unbidden, Elketh's hand went to her throat.

"We don't go around beheading people," the orc guard assured Elketh, but Elketh wasn't so sure. "You're making a scene."

"That crown has been through sixteen coronations," Vera said. "*Sixteen*."

"Did you bring her to—to Ruga first?" Hedda asked.

Without answering, Vera marched away. Elketh turned to the guard, flinching when she saw the expression on her face. She was angry. Fuming. Her voice had been so calm but a vein stuck out on her neck, her fists at her sides.

"I don't suppose you're going to strangle me or something," Elketh said. "I would prefer if you didn't."

The elaborate door at the end of the hallway opened. A slight human with short hair stuck her head out.

"Hedda? What's going on?" the human asked, in a sing-songy tone that surprised Elketh. Most humans were not so elegant in Elketh's experience.

"Nothing the queen has to concern herself with," Hedda said, and grabbed Elketh's arm the way she'd grabbed Vera's.

Elketh was dragged all the way back down the stairs and then shoved up against the wall by the guard. She closed her eyes against the guard's wrath. "Where's Ruga?" Hedda asked, her tone laced with malice.

"How should I know?" Elketh sputtered.

"Aren't you sleeping in her rooms?"

"She doesn't sleep there with me."

Hedda released her. If anything, the guard looked relieved.

"This isn't something that can be brushed under a rug. Did you destroy it? Where is it?" Hedda asked, taking the lead and leaving Elketh to follow or not. Elketh tripped over her feet to trail after the soldier, still massaging her earlobe.

"It's in the kitchen cellar," she said, unsure of how to get out of this. She had hoped it would be longer before it was discovered; she'd had no time to mentally prepare. "It's not, ah, pretty. Dented."

"Shit," Hedda said from twenty paces ahead of her. Elketh ran right up next to the orc and looked up at her—she was taller than Elketh, taller than Ruga, maybe as tall as the queen. Her hair was chin-length and curled around her ears and horns in a way that was almost charming, considering the brutish scar on her face.

Keep your head where it's supposed to be, Elketh, she had to remind herself, because she was still thinking about what the librarian had said about orcish tongues.

Elketh realized where Hedda was taking her only after they were back in the kitchens, passing the same staff who had watched

Vera lead Elketh out in the first place. If Queen Astrid's goal was to be subtle about Elketh not wanting to be there, Elketh had surely ruined it.

Hedda, at least, did not tug her along by the ear.

They rounded one corner and then another, and in the distance above, Elketh could make out the familiar shape of the window she looked out every day. The fragrance of the roses overwhelmed her as she kept her gaze up, up, up, and not on Ruga's surprised face.

"What is it?" Ruga asked. "What happened?"

Elketh finally looked down. Ruga had been sitting on the pretty stone bench in the middle of her rose garden, perhaps enjoying her evening before dinner. She was up now, brushing pollen from her dress.

"It's the elf," Hedda said vehemently. Elketh wondered if the guard had not deigned to learn Elketh's name. "She's destroyed the crown."

Ruga's brow furrowed. A sharp, lancing pain coursed through Elketh's torso. She didn't matter, Elketh told herself. Elketh had used people before and this was nothing new.

"Astrid's crown?" Ruga said finally.

"No. The ceremonial crown."

Ruga recoiled. "May I ask why?"

"What's a rusty crown to you people, anyway?" Elketh asked. She examined a cuticle on her hand, placing a carefully bored expression on her face. "Now you can get Queen Astrid a new one."

Hedda threw her arms up. "This is hopeless. I had no idea that you weren't getting along. We could have done something—"

"Hedda," Ruga said, and Hedda stiffened. "Who else saw this?"

"Vera," Hedda said. "Everyone in the kitchens, anyone Vera passed when she tried to turn in the elf to Astrid first, several of the queen's félag guarding her hall." And then, after a beat, she added, "And Freya."

Ruga closed her eyes. "Freya?"

"She might not have known what was going on."

"I need you to leave."

Hedda's shoulders slumped. "Are you sure you can't use my help?"

"Yes."

Stiffly, Hedda pivoted on her feet and stalked back to the castle, leaving Elketh alone with Ruga.

Ruga's face crumpled when Hedda was gone. Elketh's sharp pain became worse seeing it. The heartbroken reaction was too much to face, and she didn't understand why.

CHAPTER TWELVE

"Will you let me leave now?" Elketh asked, petulant.

Ruga could scream. She could punch the wall until her knuckles cracked. She could rip her roses from their stems and let the thorns cut through her hands. How could Elketh be so obtuse? It didn't seem possible. Ruga hated to admit how disappointed she was, hated to admit that she really fell for Elketh's act earlier that day when they'd been getting along. Very nearly, she'd almost believed she could emerge from these fifty days with a friend, if not a wife.

She took a moment to gather herself before she replied to Elketh. She tried to remember that she wouldn't want to be sent away somewhere without her permission, either. "How many times do I have to tell you that we have never kept you captive?"

That Elketh refused to make eye contact with her was a minor consolation. The elf looked unbothered, almost bored with the conversation. But if she really felt nothing, she'd have no issue making eye contact. She'd glared people down plenty of times. "I'm not allowed to leave."

"You may go wherever you like," Ruga said, keeping her tone even. "How can I help?"

"Help what?"

"Help you feel less trapped."

At this, Elketh did meet her eyes. Her plump lips parted in surprise and then twisted with the rest of her face in anger. "Are you daft? I just destroyed an important artifact to your country, and you're offering me *help* feeling *comfortable?*" Her voice got louder and louder with each word, and at the last one, she shoved Ruga in the chest.

Ruga stumbled back a step. "I think you want a rise out of me, and I don't want to give you one." The shove wasn't very hard, a fact she added to her evidence against Elketh's seeming apathy.

"That's bullshit," Elketh said. She crossed her arms over her chest. "I demand to be released."

"Where?"

"Back to Branwen."

"Who's to say your father won't send you right back here? You could try it. Try swimming, too, for an extra challenge," Ruga said before she could stop herself, because she was angry, and bitter, but she was trying not to match childishness with childishness.

Elketh huffed as she made her abrupt exit. "And send a servant to draw me a bath!" she shouted behind her.

Ruga let out a low breath—for a second, she thought Elketh might destroy her rose garden, too. Why hadn't she? Ruga had let Elketh know how important the roses were to her. It would be easy to burn them to the ground if Elketh's goal was to get on Ruga's nerves. Elketh wouldn't have ruined the heirloom unless she was trying to cause an international incident.

Exile was her motive, perhaps. But Torden didn't often exile people, or they hadn't in many years. Ruga's stomach grumbled as she sat back on the stone bench she slept on every night.

The crown didn't matter, really. If it did, it wouldn't spend all that time on display in the library. It was an ugly thing, notoriously so. What did matter was its history and what it meant to Torden as a symbol. Elketh had not destroyed a rusty old crown, as she put it, but a part of their history, the part that celebrated the first time someone was crowned based on value to the community rather than bloodlines.

This was it, then. Ruga had made too many excuses for Elketh—had been tricked by her, tricked into thinking Elketh could care—and she'd been burned. She'd been fooled by the image of Elketh at the archery range, Elketh pathetically drunk and down on her luck, images that were incongruous with someone capable of this kind of destruction. Ruga would have to distance herself. She was too soft and vulnerable. The best punishment to give Elketh was to cut her off from any more misguided attempts at understanding.

After all, Ruga was sure Elketh understood the crown's significance, symbolism or not. Ruga could only imagine how Vera had seen what Elketh had done and taken her out to be publicly drawn and quartered. The rest of the public, too, if they knew, would be upset not just with Elketh, but with Branwen itself.

Ruga couldn't let that happen.

The only thing to do was to cover up the crown's destruction as best as she could, for as long as she could, and pray Elketh had found her way out of Torden before anyone noticed.

What a great disappointment the elf was turning out to be.

Ruga spent the rest of her evening not in the great hall with the others but in the library, working with Vera to obscure a crime neither of them had committed. Vera was quiet through the whole thing, more upset even than Ruga. Ruga wondered if it was because Vera had dismissed Elketh as harmless when the elf was anything but.

"And no one is to know about this. Not the queen and especially not Freya," Ruga reminded her, not for the first time.

Vera merely grunted in response. Together, they draped a fabric over the whole display case. Not many people ventured to this part of the library, but every year, historians from all over Torden gathered in Vakker for the autumn history fair to celebrate Torden's culture and argue over scholarly accuracies Ruga cared little for. Many of them came to see the crown itself in appreciation of its historical significance.

The missing heirloom would be noticed eventually. It was just a matter of when.

Ruga swept up the remains of the crown under the pretense of checking on the kitchens. Several people inquired about the spectacle Vera caused. Even with her frustrations, Ruga could hardly blame Vera for reacting that way. It was a good thing Hedda had been there to stop Vera from bothering the queen. Who knew what action Astrid would want to take against Elketh?

She had the shards of the crown in a cloth sack over her shoulder by the time Freya came to investigate.

Ruga was not sure she'd ever heard the queen's maid's footsteps before, only that Freya appeared out of nowhere, as though she had been there all along. Likely, she had. Freya was shorter than most of the orcs, as humans tended to be, with close-cropped hair, and she was dressed in her customary brown tunic and trousers. Most people didn't look at her twice.

They didn't know any better.

"Freya," Ruga said, as pleasantly as she could make her voice sound.

"Ruga," Freya said, and tapped her shoulder. "What have you got there?"

"Trash. I was taking it out."

"That's a rather nice bag for trash, don't you think?" Freya asked with a knowing smile. She didn't expect Ruga to answer because Freya knew Ruga was lying. Freya seemed to know everything. The staff said she had eyes in the back of her head and ears in every room. It was nearly true. "A little bird told me that your elf fiancée came into the kitchens and stole some kitchen equipment, then holed herself up in the cellar until Vera forcefully removed her."

"Is that so."

"You don't know what that's about?"

"Absolutely not."

"And it has nothing to do with what's in the bag?" Freya asked, leaning forward like she could see through the fabric.

"It has nothing to do with the contents of this bag," Ruga confirmed. Freya's observant gaze swept up and down Ruga's body, scanning for secrets. Fear spiked in Ruga's heart. Freya could sniff out a lie a mile away.

"Why did Vera bring Elketh to the queen's rooms?" Freya asked. "If you don't tell me, I'll find out some other way."

Vera had been very close to telling Astrid, anyway, despite Ruga's protests. Freya would not have to interrogate Vera very hard to discover the truth.

"Can't you accept that it's better not to know some things?"

"Never," Freya said.

"It's personal. Between me and Elketh. We're working through some things."

"Romantic things?"

"I wouldn't get your hopes up." Ruga shifted the bag to her other shoulder, self-conscious of the sound of clanking metal. "Speaking of, is there news from Branwen?"

"We heard from the king this morning. He says he doesn't want to see her again unless she's on your arm. Our last letter made him aware that it put us in a stressful position to host someone who has no desire to engage in a political alliance. We can't hide that from people forever." Freya took another step toward Ruga. "There are rumors already."

Whatever rumors the seamstress had spread didn't do much, then. "That's not exactly surprising, considering her attitude toward the staff." Ruga would have to sneak in again and draw another bath, even though she hardly thought Elketh deserved it.

"You seemed chummy with her at the training grounds," Freya pointed out, and it was no surprise that she knew.

"I think she was trying to use me for something," Ruga admitted. Putting her guard down, maybe, to set up this whole thing.

Freya nodded. "If you don't have anything else to share with me, I'll be on my way."

"Wait, Freya," Ruga said. Freya was halfway down the hall. It was a bad time to bring it up, but there might not be another chance. "I sent the ceremonial crown away to be cleaned."

Freya's nostrils flared. "Where did you send it?"

"Place between Torden and Lynby," Ruga said, scrambling to think of an existing business that would pass one of Freya's meticulous checks. "A friend of Vera's, a trusted preserver of old artifacts. He'll be discreet."

It wouldn't take long for Freya to figure out she was lying, but whatever time Ruga could buy was good time. "I see," said Freya.

CHAPTER THIRTEEN

The first thing Elketh did when she got to her rooms was check on the status of her bath. She had been looking forward to raging if she was unable to take one; to her dismay, steam rose from the hot water in the large tub. Elketh settled herself into the bath, her skin crying for relief, her rapid breaths becoming regular again after the stress of the day. She had not eaten, and no one had left her food. This was likely the last bath she would have to take in Torden.

Later, Elketh paced her rooms back and forth with dripping hair, waiting for a punishment that didn't come. When she was too tired to walk, she stubbornly sat in the chair by Ruga's writing desk and waited some more until she had fallen asleep.

Far too early the next morning, Elketh woke to a crick in her neck and the damned sun in her face. She groggily leaned out the window, telling herself she was listening for the bustle of an elvish retinue arriving to retrieve her, or at the very least orcish soldiers coming to expel her. All she heard was the chirping of summer doves. She stood over the window, fingers curling over the stone, for a minute more before she allowed herself to look down into the rose garden.

She did not find what she wanted to see.

Fuming, she brushed her hair—an activity she looked forward to a servant doing for her as soon as she got home—and dressed in one of the nicer dresses, waiting for someone to bring her news.

The only person who came brought her breakfast instead. The kitchens had given up on preparing elvish food. This was one of the concessions they had made without asking, and Elketh did not particularly care about adhering to an elvish diet over an orcish one. But the diet change gave her the perfect excuse to throw a fit. She yelled at the kitchen boy who brought the tray just for something to do, and when he ran down the hall without fighting back, she sank into the bed, bouncing her knee.

The noises in the castle were painfully normal, devoid of panic. If Ruga had somehow obscured the crown's destruction, Elketh would throw a bigger fit, maybe burn something down this time. It had to be public and obvious.

She expected that Ruga would come to her rooms to get more clothes or to express how angry she was with her. Elketh played out the scene in her head: how she would tell Ruga she hated her and her stupid country, how she hardly thought anyone with cute little mouth tusks could be taken seriously, and therefore, she couldn't feel bad about ruining some old piece of metal kept behind glass. She rehearsed her responses with all the devotion of an actress in a play.

The sun rose higher in the sky and then began its descent. No one came to see Elketh.

In the early afternoon, when she could no longer stand it, Elketh left her rooms. She glanced left and then right down the hall—there was not even a guard there to keep her company or serve as the victim of her next tantrum. Grumbling, she descended the stairs, passing several servants who hardly spared her a glance, and made her way outside, following the trail to the archery range.

She selected a crossbow from the weapon racks and a quiver of bolts. Two orcs watched her as she made her way to an open space in the center rather than the secluded clearing Ruga had taken her to.

Elketh nocked the first bolt and released it. The bolt collided with the first target with such force that the wood cracked. It was satisfying to destroy something, but she liked the longbow more. She set the next bolt in place and repeated the action, again and again, until her arms burned from pulling back the string, until the thwacking of arrows around her stopped and she felt all eyes on her in the clearing. She did it until she was out of bolts, and then basked in the impressed faces of the orcs.

Any pride she felt dissipated at once. There was only one orc Elketh wanted to impress, and she wasn't here.

Elketh stalked back to her rooms, sweaty and feeling worse than ever, to find that someone had left a fresh tray of food by the door and drawn her another bath. She eased sore muscles into the hot water with the impression that she was a character from the old myths with invisible servants, a mortal punished by the goddess for her own arrogance by living forever alone. Or maybe she was in the myth where her servant was invisible, but if she caught sight of their true appearance, she would lose them.

She had trouble remembering if it was really a servant that the woman in the myth had seen or someone else.

Dressed in just a robe, she peered out her door to discover someone had left her a tray of food without giving her the chance to yell at them. She threw Ruga's inkpot at the wall. Black ink splattered over the tally marks she'd made to count the passage of the days.

That night, Elketh tossed and turned, but the next morning was no different—no signs of anyone coming to get her, and no signs of anyone coming to kick her out, either. She remembered what Ruga said about being free to leave, but where would she go, if not home? She hardly wanted to visit the other islands, and she didn't have connections anywhere else.

The first change came with the delivery of her breakfast. It was brought by a guard. Elketh eyed the plate—orcish food only—warily, because she wasn't sure if the guard was sent in response to her treatment of the kitchen servants, or whether she'd be beaten for putting up a fight.

"Ruga says," the guard said, and Elketh suddenly recognized her, "not to yell at the staff, and that this is your last warning."

It was the guard who had prevented Elketh from being surrendered to the queen. Herring, or something like that. "Do you have news from my father?" Elketh asked.

The guard grimaced as she set down the tray without being told. In Branwen, that would be borderline insolence. "He doesn't want you back until you've agreed to marry Ruga." There was a tightness in her voice that set Elketh on edge.

"Why did you stop Vera from giving me over to the queen?" Elketh asked.

Herring jabbed a finger at Elketh. "The queen has more important things to worry about than a bratty elf."

Bratty, Elketh thought to herself as she chewed through some bread alone. It was a word she'd been called before, though she never took it seriously because no one really cared if the heir to an Elven Island was bratty. It was part of the job. She wondered if the word applied to her now.

The bread did not sit well, nor did the fish, nor did the porridge. Elketh ran a finger over the rim of the bowl. Seventeen days. Seventeen days ago, her father had dropped her off here and left her at the whims of the orcs without bothering to obtain Elketh's input. No matter how stubborn she was, her father wouldn't budge, and no matter how many times she offended people in the castle or destroyed their precious artifacts, she was still stuck here. Elketh was positive that if there were news to bring her, it would have happened by now. It was just like her father to not give in to her.

But maybe the orcs did not quite deserve her obstinacy.

The thought slithered in and took hold until Elketh felt quite feverish from it. Elketh wrapped herself in Ruga's covers, which still smelled like the orc even after several weeks of Elketh sleeping in them. Seventeen days down, and thirty-three to go, if she was to wait out her time here. There was no way she'd actually marry an orc—she still had her heart set on Rhiannon—but if she waited it out just a month or so, she could return home and say that they were incompatible, at the very least, and demand a new consort. A month was nothing to someone whose life expectancy was upward of eight hundred years. But then, time worked differently in Torden, expanding into an eternity.

In the late afternoon, Elketh pried herself from her sheets and made herself presentable. She braided her hair and splashed her face with water. She changed into a slim, unadorned dress that was not her style at all.

And then she set out for the great hall.

The guard standing by the building's entrance expressed surprise at seeing her. Elketh gave him an impish smile. She loved to be unpredictable.

When the guard opened the door for her, the sounds of chatter and clinking pottery stopped in time with the creaking of the hinges.

Elketh was the center of attention. She straightened her back and smiled at the crowd. The skald, reciting a story of heroes of old, overcame her hesitation and started back up again, the only voice in the room. Elketh stood there, soaking in the orcs' reactions until her eyes met Ruga's. Her expression was unreadable.

Daintily lifting her dress so it didn't drag, Elketh stepped up the stairs to the raised dais where people close to the queen sat. She nodded to the queen as she passed her. The queen's eyes followed Elketh, free of the judgment that would come with knowing what Elketh had done.

Ruga kept her head down, facing her half-eaten plate, when Elketh got close. Across the room, chatter trickled back into the hall. Elketh stopped behind her. The orc that had been sitting next to Ruga moved a spot down on the bench. A guard swept an unused plate from the next table over and set it in place for Elketh.

In a rush of adrenaline, Elketh eased her hand over Ruga's shoulder. Muscles tensed under her fingers. She moved her hand, brushing Ruga's hair out of the way. Ever-so-slightly, Ruga turned her head, a question forming on her lips. Whatever she'd been about to ask died as Elketh pressed a light kiss to Ruga's cheek.

The rest of the hall went back to its pre-Elketh chatter, but everyone at their table was focused on Elketh and Ruga. These people, Elketh thought, were likelier to know the truth of the matter. The idea of confusing them delighted her.

"You two are getting along well, aren't you?" an orc in a flouncy dress asked from across the table. An earl of some kind. To their left, Herring grunted.

"Oh, yes," Elketh said, and served herself food the way she'd seen the orcs do on her first night there. "I'm very fond of Ruga."

Elketh basked in all the *awwws* that resonated down the table. She drank mead and forced herself to be polite, answering questions as they came her way and laughing when appropriate.

Next to her, Ruga was abnormally quiet. It wasn't until someone told a loud story at the opposite end of the room that Ruga finally spoke.

"What are you doing?" Ruga asked under her breath, pushing around the same food on her plate that had been there twenty minutes ago.

Elketh considered ignoring her, but she was desperate to know what Ruga was thinking. "Changing tactics," Elketh said honestly.

"And what," said Ruga, "is your goal?"

"I'm playing along. Like you wanted."

"You've never cared about what I wanted before."

That was true. "I'm having a change of heart."

Ruga tapped her knife against her plate, a tad too loud. "Are you?"

Elketh was less sure about the truth of that. It made her uneasy to think about. "Can we talk after dinner?"

The skald finished her poem and left, which was the signal for everyone who was only there for the meal to exit politely. Ruga didn't answer. Once again, Elketh felt her stomach churning as Ruga stood with the rest of the queen's retinue and exited the hall.

CHAPTER FOURTEEN

Ruga bit her lip so hard that she tasted blood. She was in a foul mood. The rose garden would be a rough place to sleep tonight—all day long, people commented on the looming rain clouds, and during dinner, the skies had opened. The ground would be wet, and she'd get no sleep at all. She considered the effort it would take to find some place uninhabited in the castle that wasn't monitored by guards—and whether it was worth hiding it, still, since now some of the guards, or at least Hedda, certainly knew things weren't going as planned—and that frustrated her more.

That was only the first thing gone wrong today.

She couldn't comprehend Elketh's agenda. The elf had gone and ruined the crown in a clear attempt to sabotage not only the Torden orcs but also any relationship she could have had with them. Ruga needed to get away, but her rooms were taken, her favorite places outdoors. It would be so embarrassing to tell her sister she needed a place to sleep. It was bad enough that she had to get ready every morning in the queen's rooms.

Deep in thought, she had fallen behind the rest of the queen's retinue that shielded her from having to deal with Elketh. Ruga didn't notice someone drag her into an alcove until it had already happened. In the dying light of the day, she looked into a breathtaking face.

"Ruga," Elketh said, and Ruga hated how much she liked the sound of her name in Elketh's voice. The alcove was small, and the two had to stand close to fit.

"What do you want?" Ruga said.

Elketh flinched. Guilt crawled up Ruga's spine. "I shouldn't have done that," Elketh said.

"Which part?" Ruga imagined Elketh's lips soft against her cheek.

"Ruining your heirloom," Elketh said. "I shouldn't have done it."

"And?"

"And I'm very sorry."

Ruga scrutinized Elketh's expression. Tears lined the elf's lower lashes.

But tears could be faked.

Elketh cleared her throat. "I have a question for you."

Ruga became aware of how close they were. Stepping back would make it obvious that their proximity was on her mind.

"Why did you cover for me?"

"I didn't cover for *you*," Ruga said. "I covered up the destruction of an important part of our history so it wouldn't upset my sister. I covered it so that our country wouldn't go to war with your island." She took a breath, collecting herself, and brushed against Elketh's arm, trying to shift positions. "Your people would lose, by the way."

"I know that," Elketh said, small. "I thought maybe..."

"Maybe what? I would cover up your crime just so my people didn't rise up and tear you limb from limb?"

"Do you really think they would do that?"

"Metaphorically."

"I'm not talking metaphors," Elketh said, leaning close enough that Ruga could smell the mead on her breath. "I just thought helping me might have something to do with it, too, that's all."

"If it did, and I'm not saying it did," said Ruga, "there are many reasons I would cover up such a thing before you ever became one of them."

Elketh nodded. "All right. Whatever your reasons, my apology stands."

Inching her way back, Ruga said, "Where does that leave us?"

"Ah—acquaintances, I suppose. Or something short of rivals."

Ruga stiffened. "I didn't mean our relationship. Are you going to continue to sabotage Astrid's court? I will find a way to stop you if you do. We can't have a weakness within the castle walls."

"I meant my apology. I'm not going to do that kind of thing anymore. I had some time to think."

"A verbal apology means nothing to me. You'll have to show me you mean it," said Ruga, feeling bitter. She wished that this whole situation could be avoided, that the elf could be returned home, that she had never come here in the first place.

Elketh took a deep breath. "What if I told you that I'm really mad at my father, but I've been taking it out on Torden?"

Was she serious? "I would say that you're telling me what I want to hear."

"I'm going to wait out the fifty days," Elketh said, which was about the last thing Ruga expected. "We can argue with my father after, but it seems he doesn't want to negotiate until the betrothal period has passed."

Ruga leaned back against the window. "Hedda's talked to you, I suppose."

"Is that her name? I keep thinking it's Herring."

Ruga snorted. She looked away from her reflection in the window back at Elketh, who wore a smug smile. Seeing it made Ruga's stomach flip. *Distance yourself,* Ruga reminded herself. *What happened to distancing yourself?*

"Come with me," she said impulsively.

Elketh's thin eyebrows rose. "Where to?"

But Ruga kept her in suspense as they trailed out of the castle and into the rain. Her dress became heavy with droplets. Their destination wasn't far, and Elketh made no complaint as she trudged through the rain behind Ruga.

The blacksmith's forge glowed in contrast with the dark windows of the businesses around it. They'd be shut to the public, the blacksmith closing up shop for the day. Ruga entered the establishment to find the blacksmith orc hunched over an anvil, her fingernails rimmed with dirt.

"Hello," the blacksmith said when she saw Ruga, and then a more formal, "Welcome," when Elketh stepped in behind her. The blacksmith dabbed at sweat on her forehead with a cloth. "I'm about to finish up here."

"Do you mind if I stick around?" Ruga asked, though she knew the answer even before the blacksmith nodded. She led Elketh to a corner with a stool and a series of small tools. "Sit," Ruga said, and Elketh sat on the stool. Ruga made herself at home on the floor, rummaging through the baskets underneath the bench for her project.

She found the one she was looking for. With one hand, she ran fingers through the pile of loose chainmail links she'd painstakingly severed from a coil.

"Do you forgive me?" Elketh asked as Ruga located the basket that held the beginnings of her latest project. It wasn't a question Ruga knew the answer to. She'd wanted Elketh to ask about the craft itself, like she had with the roses.

"I don't think so," said Ruga. She lifted the small sheet of mail, holding it to the dim light of the window, just close enough to Elketh's lap that the elf could interpret it as an offer to examine closer. Elketh accepted the mesh sheet in her hands, tugging at the links to test their steadfastness.

"Why do you want me around, then?"

Ruga began to loop links through each other with quick fingers, closing them shut with a tool from the bench. "Do you find it hard to keep quiet?" she countered.

"Yes," said Elketh. "Do you find it hard to talk about your feelings?"

"Almost never." Ruga nudged the bench closer to herself and hung the chainmail off of two nails. "To answer questions you haven't asked, or maybe don't care about, the blacksmith lets me work on this here. One of my many skills. Or hobbies, as you put it."

Elketh didn't respond to this right away. Ruga glanced up from her work and found that Elketh had come quite close, leaning down nearly as far as she could without falling off the stool. Her near-black eyes glittered with mirth. "If I didn't know any better, I would think you *wanted* my attention."

"Why would I bring you here," said Ruga, "if not to observe me?"

Elketh's mouth curved at that. A glimmer of satisfaction bloomed in Ruga's chest. She liked that she knew the elf enough to guess that Elketh would appreciate a challenge. "All right. I can play. Why chainmail?"

Ruga pulled the chainmail taut. "There was a human blacksmith from the north who traveled through Vakker to trade his wares. He showed me how to make it."

"That doesn't answer why."

"Chainmail takes hours—years, even—to assemble. And it's a repetitive task that keeps my hands busy. My mind always feels clear when I do it."

"I suppose that explains the giant sheet of it on your bedchamber wall."

"Yes. That took me nearly two decades to finish."

For a moment, the blacksmith sweeping up on the other side of the shop was the only thing they had to fill the silence. Then: "Do you always make plain rectangular sheets, or do you make them fitted for people?"

Ruga suppressed a smile. "I do either. I've sold a few hauberks fitted for humans, though I don't like contributing to their wars. Of course, it's more about the task itself than its usage. Astrid's standard requires us to use rivets to make them extra secure. And the guards in her félag have protective magic woven into theirs. I don't have the patience for rivets."

"You have a lot of hobbies for a princess."

"I'm surprised you don't have more," Ruga said. The mail grew steadily under her touch. "It's boring to fill time with the same thing over and over again. We're always picking up new things. It's how my sister became queen." She assumed Elketh did not know of the heroic feat that had gotten Astrid unanimously elected as Torden's ruler.

Elketh's dress rustled as she shifted. "The throne isn't passed to the firstborn child like on the Elven Islands," Elketh said, maybe more to herself than Ruga. "It's based on who is the most skilled?"

"It's a bit more complicated than that, but yes."

"So you are a seamstress, a gardener, and a blacksmith. What else? A cobbler?"

The nails strained at the table. The mail was becoming too heavy for them. "It's getting dark. Light a candle?"

"A tanner?" Elketh asked as she rummaged through metal scraps for a tallow candle. "Weaver?"

"I like to carve wood, too," Ruga said as she adjusted the mail. She settled back on the ground and looped another link through two others, then clamped it closed. "And I wove the tapestry in the dining hall with the dancing women. Put that on the list."

"But not archery," Elketh said, positing the lit candle in a rare spot of free space on the bench. Instead of returning to her stool, she sat on the dirt floor with Ruga. Their knees nearly touched. "I can hold it."

"Not archery," Ruga confirmed. "Nor am I a swordswoman, nor a hunter."

"Why would you need to be, if you don't eat meat?" The edge of the mail jingled in Elketh's lap, her hands securing the first row of links on the far left and right. It wasn't the most efficient way to keep the mail in place, but Ruga didn't say anything.

"I guess you're right. I don't have the stomach for killing animals." Elketh was watching Ruga's hands very closely, the repetitive movement with its clinking at regular intervals. "I can shear sheep, though."

"Of course you can. The court skald should write you into a poem."

The corners of Ruga's eyes crinkled. "She has."

"What's it about?"

Ruga squeezed another link of mail shut with iron pliers. "It's too raunchy to share."

The entire sheet fell to the dirt in a shiver of metal as Elketh nudged Ruga on the bicep, playful. "Ruga!"

"It was just a little fling," Ruga said. Normally, she would be annoyed by dropping the mail, but her mood was considerably lighter than it had been. She retrieved it, brushing off dirt and hay from the ground. "I don't do flings often."

"I do," Elketh said, sitting back and giving up all pretense of helping Ruga. "I miss them. I haven't had sex in..."

"Seventeen days?"

"Seventeen days." Elketh quirked an eyebrow at Ruga. "How'd you know?"

"Lucky guess," Ruga said. "You're flirty and impatient." And attractive; Ruga doubted Elketh had problems finding partners.

"Impatient?"

"You haven't sat still since I brought you here."

"You must be ultra-patient," Elketh said. "All your hobbies are arduous. They require a lot of focus."

"I like things that keep my thoughts quiet." But Ruga kept herself busy, too, kept her hands busy and kept her mind busy, regardless of intent. "What else would you tell me about yourself if we were going through with the marriage? Other than about your amorous escapades."

"That's all there is to me," Elketh said, grinning, and Ruga couldn't help but grin back. Stars. She understood how Elketh found her lovers—Elketh was playing Ruga right into the palm of her hand, and Ruga was falling for it almost gladly.

"Really, though," Ruga said. "I actually want to know."

Uncomfortable, Elketh glanced downward. "What is there to know? I'm a spoiled princess. Born to privilege with the expectation that I would one day rule and get to do whatever I wanted. I'm very similar to my father."

"Somehow, I doubt that."

"Why?"

"Would you abandon your daughter to strangers?"

Elketh was quiet. "No," she said at last. "I suppose not. Though if the stranger is you, my imaginary daughter would be lucky."

"You're buttering me up again," Ruga accused, and still she fell for it.

"Yes."

"Okay, well. Do you want to talk about your relationship to your father? It seems...different than I'm used to."

Elketh made an annoyed face. "He's pushy and stubborn. Always has to get his way."

"That does sound like you."

"He always had a million things for me to do," Elketh continued, huffing. "Standards to uphold. Things like that. I was so damn sick of it. He's stuffy and lives in the past. I've tried my whole life to defy him, and I still ended up here. He out-stubborned me."

Ruga paused, sensing that this was the closest to honesty Elketh had ever been. Of course Elketh would have turned out so obstinate if she was raised in those circumstances. Ruga's childhood had been so different from hers. Being part of a royal family hadn't even entered the picture until half a century ago. She'd had quite a few freedoms as a merchants' daughter.

Ruga thought to share her story with Elketh, but she lost her grip on the pliers when Elketh placed a hand over hers.

"Not that I don't like chatting with you," Elketh said, "but why are we here?"

Elketh was bent over Ruga. Ruga's throat was suddenly very dry. "I am trying to forgive you. You said you would be here for another month."

"And it's too much effort to hate me?"

Noncommittally, Ruga grunted. There was another reason for it: she simply liked Elketh. Days ago, she had accepted this. For whatever reason, Ruga was soft on Elketh, unbearably soft to the point of gullibility. After the crown incident, she'd resolved herself to not show Elketh kindness, but today... It was hard to explain. There were traits of Elketh's that Ruga admired. Elketh stood up for herself, for one. Ruga would never forget how Elketh jumped into the harbor just to get away from her perceived captors. The elf was bold and stubborn and perfectly capable of taking care of herself, no matter how much she pretended that she needed someone to bring her the right food or draw her baths.

Even the destruction of the crown was an example of Elketh's being headstrong. She had ruined it in an attempt to free herself, something she'd only resorted to when there appeared to be no other options. Ruga had obsessed over Elketh all night, and she'd finally come to a strange conclusion: It hurt Ruga more that Elketh had disregarded her feelings than that she had taken a hammer to the crown.

"Yes. It's too much effort to hate you," Ruga said.

CHAPTER FIFTEEN

It wasn't until late the next day that Elketh understood Ruga's change of heart.

At breakfast—Elketh attended this time without being asked—the two sat next to each other on the bench. This was their first normal meal together. Elketh was careful to participate in the conversation, as she had the night before. Everyone seemed to be warming up to her except for Hedda, who sat at the queen's side sullenly in her leather armor.

The skald recited a story in flowery verse about a beautiful maiden who fell in love with an artist, and Elketh nudged Ruga in the side, raising her eyebrows.

"Is this the one about you?"

Ruga smirked behind her ale. "This is much too chaste to be about me."

"How scandalous."

"I'm sure you've done worse back home."

Elketh gave Ruga a light elbow to the ribs, and Ruga laughed. Hedda scowled at them. Elketh supposed not everyone was as kind as Ruga. What she did had been pretty severe, and rubbing it in

Hedda's face that she wasn't facing any punishment seemed like a recipe for sending the guard running to the queen to profess the truth.

Even with that hanging over her head, it was nice to flirt again. Elketh always felt at her best when she could be playful. She was grateful that Ruga was willing to indulge her.

After breakfast, Elketh planned to go to the archery range. If she was going to be stuck here, she was going to make the most of it. Whenever she got back to Branwen, she planned to commission a place to practice like the training grounds near Vakker Castle.

She never got the chance to go.

To her surprise, Ruga stopped her outside the dining hall. "You've been cooped up in your room for a lot of the time since you arrived," Ruga said. "I want you to see what I contribute here."

"Will you be painting portraits?" Elketh suggested. "I'm happy to pose nude."

Ruga rolled her eyes, but she was smiling. "Unfortunately, it's a lot more diplomatic than that."

She had a written list of people to visit. It wasn't in her handwriting. Not that Elketh paid a lot of attention to what Ruga's handwriting looked like, or had parsed through the papers on her writing desk or anything. "I'm pretending we're in love to everyone?" Elketh asked, realizing they were going door-to-door.

"I doubt anyone expects us to be in love," Ruga said. "Just getting along. The only thing you're pretending is that you still intend to marry me."

It was a relief to hear Ruga talk like she didn't mean for the alliance to happen. Elketh followed her, quickly growing bored, as Ruga went around town, knocking on doors of businesses and homes alike. Several of the people they visited were in sour moods when Ruga got there, only to be appeased by a bag of coin or a gift.

Even though the task was tedious, Elketh was eager to participate and prove how much she meant her apology. She did not apologize often. Ruga had Elketh carry a sack of goods that became significantly lighter as they went on.

Some of the orcs wanted to see Elketh up close, especially the older ones, who maintained little to no sense of personal space. One of them squeezed her cheeks, spreading her mouth open to check the state of her teeth as Ruga held back laughter. "When you've lived for a thousand years, you stop caring what people think of you," Ruga proposed as an explanation.

"I think they're hazing me," Elketh said, massaging the side of her face.

A pattern emerged. Whenever Ruga showed up, whatever the person she came to visit was troubled by when Ruga first arrived was alleviated by the end. Elketh began to understand Ruga's role in Torden. She was a friendly face for people to complain to. Occasionally, she took notes as people talked and assured them that whatever concerns they had would be a top priority, even when they seemed to Elketh like the smallest thing ever. Who cared about who was seated where for the upcoming midsummer celebration? Some even brought minor disputes to Ruga, complaining for nearly half an hour of a neighbor grinding grain in their quern at early hours.

"I'll talk to them," Ruga promised, and she did when they stopped at the next house. She danced around words until the neighbor understood what she was asking and ended up gifting her a half-empty bottle of mead for it.

"They love you," Elketh said to Ruga when they'd left. "How did you learn to talk like that?"

Ruga looked tired. "My sister has been queen for fifty-two years," she said. "I have been doing this for a while."

"That list was people who were unhappy with something?" Elketh asked. "Where did you get it?"

"I'm not spilling state secrets to you," Ruga said, with a playful air Elketh liked. "As you can see, not all of them are as serious as others. But it looks good that I go investigate them all."

"You do this every day?" Elketh asked.

Ruga stopped at a street stall and gave the seller way too much money for a carton of boiled herring and another of roasted nuts. She handed the herring to Elketh, who accepted it gratefully. Elketh munched down on the fish as they walked.

"Not every day," Ruga said. "About once a week."

"And they were going to give you away to Branwen? Who else would do this when you left?" But even as she said it, she realized how meaningful the alliance really was.

Ruga, a diplomatic figure and a friendly face with deep ties to the royal family, made time in her day to talk to the everyday people. In Branwen, no one served this kind of role. But Ruga would have done it there, too. What a gift the orcs intended to give the island elves. Elketh wondered if her father knew the depth of the marriage alliance, of Ruga's character, or what his motive had been in trying to ally them. Ruga would have offered Branwen, Elketh felt, more than Branwen had to offer Torden, even if Branwen supplied Torden with an entire army.

"We would have found someone," Ruga said, a bit tightly.

"I see the value in it," Elketh said. "Having someone accessible to listen to everyone's concerns."

Ruga looked at Elketh like she'd never seen her before. A warm flush started over Elketh's skin. Elketh would have to be dense not to notice how many times Ruga snuck glances at her throughout the day. She wished she'd worn a dress that accentuated her features rather than the tunic and trousers she'd chosen for the archery range. At the very least, Elketh was thankful she'd had the foresight to braid her hair prettily into a crown.

They passed a jeweler on the way to the next disgruntled shopkeeper. Elketh froze at the window. Several intricately carved armbands were on display. "Can we go in?" she asked.

"Do you have money to buy something?"

Elketh only had the clothes on her back when she was left in Torden. She scowled.

"I'm kidding. We have time to look around."

The back of the shop held a blacksmith forge, and the front was entirely a jewelry display area. A gruff-looking orc with dirt on her face came in and out of the main room, bringing new coiled metals for the daintier shopkeeper. The dainty orc was covered in jewelry, wearing multiple neckbands, several armbands, and even rings on her fingers. She had metal intertwined with her plaited hair. Elketh thought the effect very beautiful.

"How are you today?" Ruga asked the dainty shopkeeper as Elketh looked through the merchandise—elaborate brooches, twining patterns to ornament hair and skin. Elketh overheard enough of their conversation to glean that the blacksmith and jeweler were a couple, putting their skills together to run the shop. The blacksmith did the rougher work, and the jeweler finessed the details.

"You have a good eye," Ruga said as they left. "They're widely considered the finest jewelers in Torden."

Elketh adjusted her new neckband. It looked like the branches of a tree, stretching out over the expanse of her neck, with a rough center of amber. "Thank you for the gift." She got the impression that if she asked Ruga for other things, she would get them, but she didn't want to wrongly take advantage.

Later that afternoon, after several more houses where Elketh was prodded like cattle, Ruga brought her to a spring. The day was getting hotter as it went on and had reached its peak. Gratefully, Elketh removed her boots and rolled up her trousers to the knee, dipping her legs in the cool water.

"Please tell me that's the last of it," Elketh said as Ruga rinsed her face.

"That's the last of it," Ruga affirmed.

Elketh leaned back on her hands in the grass, trailing her feet lazily in the water. "Do you like doing all that?" she asked, her eyes closed in bliss.

"I'm good at it."

"That's hardly the same thing."

There was the sound of shuffling fabric. Then a splash. Elketh opened her eyes to find Ruga in the pool of water in just her smallclothes.

Ruga splashed an arc of water at Elketh's leg. "I like doing things that help make my sister's life easier. If that means I have to make time to talk to people when I don't feel like it, I can put up with that." She dunked her head under the surface. Elketh closed her eyes before she could allow herself to gawk at the orc's appealing figure. The glistening muscle on Ruga's bare arms caused a sweet ache between her legs.

"You would be a good consort," Elketh said before she could think better of it. Their day hadn't been fun, exactly, but it had been enjoyable to an extent. At some point, Elketh had forgotten that she didn't intend to go through with the marriage. Even with the diplomatic bits, Elketh wouldn't have minded, necessarily, spending more time with Ruga. The thought startled her.

"What makes you say that?" Ruga asked.

Elketh opened her eyes. Near her in the water, Ruga floated, just her head and shoulders above the surface, wet hair plastered back and tangled with her horns. Elketh had a strong urge to reach out and touch one of Ruga's tusks just to know what it felt like.

"I've been living in the castle, and I hardly see Queen Astrid," Elketh said. As she had been all day, Ruga was giving Elketh her full attention. And Elketh noticed Ruga noticing her and liked it. Having Ruga's attention was like having Elketh's skin kissed by the lazy afternoon sun, warm and welcoming. "I've seen plenty of you, even when I didn't mean to. Everyone recognizes you and knows you. You've wrestled bitter neighbors into friends just today. The queen may be the ruler here, but you're the face of her reign. You're invaluable to these people."

"That's kind of you to say."

Elketh averted her eyes as Ruga emerged from the water and donned her dress. She thought she should have avoided looking longer, however, as Ruga bent down and wrung out her hair to the side, muscles shifting under her clothes. The sun caught her from behind, haloing her outline like a personal message from the goddess. Subconsciously, Elketh raised a hand to her sternum and rubbed it, trying to restore the air in her lungs.

They found a place to eat: a tavern classier than the one Elketh had run away to her first day. If they tried to make it back to the castle, they'd have missed dinner. Ruga comfortably ate her stew with just her fingers and a knife, and Elketh adjusted to the abnormal way of eating—not even at Vakker Castle had she eaten with her hands. The stew was good, at least, and Elketh was appreciative the tavern had hearty options for both of their diets.

The meal restored a bit of her energy after the long day of walking. Her feet were sore, and she'd be glad to crawl back into bed.

Like she had earlier, Ruga watched Elketh with the intensity of someone who couldn't look away. Elketh found herself pushing her hair over one shoulder, giving Ruga a full glimpse of her good side (the left one), and gently wiping her fingers on a cloth instead of licking the stew off them as Ruga was. When Elketh discerned that she was doing these things, she became annoyed with herself, but not enough to stop.

They ended the day in Ruga's rose garden, with Elketh cooling off in the shade provided by a hedge, resting in the grass, and Ruga sitting on the bench, swinging her legs slowly in the breeze.

Fatigue pulled at Elketh's eyes. She didn't want to be the one to say goodbye first. The last dregs of sunset faded from the sky.

"Going around town on my sister's behalf isn't my favorite task," Ruga said after a period of comfortable silence. "I think I actually enjoyed myself today, though you probably found it dull."

Elketh wound her fingers around the grass to give herself something to do. "It wasn't so bad," she said. Admitting that she also enjoyed herself seemed awfully close to confessing to something she didn't have the words for yet.

"Thank you for joining me," Ruga said.

"Do you forgive me yet?" Elketh asked, weaving the strands of grass together.

In that husky way of hers, Ruga laughed. The sound was growing on Elketh. "I think I can get there," said Ruga.

A revelation clicked into place.

Elketh dropped the grass. "We'd better head in, don't you think?" Elketh sat up, but Ruga made no move to leave, looking down at her clasped hands.

Elketh observed the flattened grass at Ruga's feet and then Ruga.

"I have been sleeping out here," Ruga confessed.

Stupidly, Elketh's mouth dropped open. She closed it with a snap. "Outside? With the bugs and the mud? Why not in the castle somewhere?"

"I didn't want anyone to see me," Ruga said in a smallish voice, "because then they would know... You know."

They would know Elketh and Ruga were not getting along, that the marriage wasn't happening. "That's absurd."

Ruga shrugged.

"You always look so nice. How do you get ready in the morning? Where do you get dressed?"

"My sister's rooms," Ruga said. "I try to wake up early enough that it's not super noticeable. But I do get grass stains on my face." There was a pause, and then: "You think I look nice?"

"I meant you're put-together," Elketh said, cheeks burning. "I can't believe you let me sleep in your rooms when you had nowhere else to go."

"You were the one who insisted on staying there without me," Ruga said, though not meanly.

Guilt crept over Elketh. This was something she could fix. "Come sleep in your rooms tonight, then. I won't have you staying out here."

"Where will you sleep?"

Elketh stood and held out a hand to help Ruga up from the stone bench. "We'll figure it out."

CHAPTER SIXTEEN

It was turning out to be a lovely day. Ruga was glad she had thought to invite Elketh—something she'd always thought laborious was made genuinely fun, more fun even than gossiping about centuries-old drama with the older weavers as they worked at their looms together. Already, Ruga knew she would be sad to see Elketh go, despite all the trouble she'd caused. Elketh had assigned value to the house calls, had filled Ruga with appreciation for Astrid's idea to do it at all, and now she saw the grueling task in a new light.

Ruga liked that she could be changed by people in this way. Even as a woman of solitude, she cherished that her life could transform over and over again during its course through her connections to other people. The connection she'd made with Elketh was unexpected—but then, many things about Elketh were.

The castle was quiet upon their return, suspended in that liminal post-dinner haze. The sky was completely dark now, sparkling with stars, and Ruga stopped at one of the mullioned windows lining the hallway to admire the moon, three-quarters full and pregnant with possibility. Something like hope fluttered in her chest.

It was so quiet that Ruga heard Elketh's uneven footsteps trotting on ahead of her, the heavy landing of one foot and the quick touchdown of the other.

"Are you hurt?" Ruga called, shattering the silence.

Elketh grunted, waiting for Ruga to catch up. "I haven't broken in the leather yet," she said, lifting a boot. "We did a lot of walking today."

"Here." Ruga maneuvered Elketh to the windowsill and gestured for her to sit down. As Elketh grimaced, Ruga bent over to unlace the new leather boots. Elketh sighed with relief as the footwear came loose.

A nasty-looking blister had formed on the side of Elketh's little toe, and another one was forming on her instep. It was probably painful. The only thing Ruga could think was that she'd never been attracted to someone's ankle before.

"How's the other one?" Ruga asked.

"Not as bad. Though it'll get there if I keep putting all my weight on it, I'm sure."

Ruga bit her lip. "We have a lot of stairs to go."

"Don't remind me."

Deftly, Ruga unlaced the other boot and handed it to Elketh. Then she turned around and knelt. "Get on."

"What?"

"On my back," Ruga said impatiently. "Unless you wanted to walk barefoot."

"This is hardly dignified," Elketh protested, but a moment later, Ruga felt Elketh's arms wind around her neck, the boots knocking into each other in Elketh's grasp.

Ruga hooked Elketh's legs on either side of her and started for the stairs. "I have a salve in my bedchamber...unless you did something to it. It should soothe your blisters," Ruga said, but it seemed like Elketh was no longer in the talking mood.

The silence was different now, pervasive, and Ruga was overly conscious of the press of Elketh against her, the nonexistent distance between their bodies.

At the door to her rooms, Ruga set Elketh down. "Thanks," Elketh said. There was an odd expression on her face, the light of the hallway lanterns dancing in her dark irises. She looked almost upset.

"Is everything all right?"

"I see the way you look at me," said Elketh.

Of course she had. Ruga had done very little to hide it, had not thought it worth hiding, because Elketh seemed like the kind of person who liked to be admired, and Ruga had wanted to give her what she liked.

"And what," said Ruga, "do you think of that?"

Elketh glanced to the end of the hall, where a guard stood sentry. "I don't know."

"Would you like to know?"

Elketh sputtered something that wasn't words.

Ruga reached for Elketh, but Elketh stepped away until her back was flush with the wall. Again, slower, Ruga reached for her, grazing Elketh's hand with her own. Elketh let Ruga take her limp hand, not pulling back even when Ruga brought it to her mouth.

"May I?" Ruga asked.

"May...you...what?" Elketh whispered.

"Kiss your hand."

A conflicted expression crossed Elketh's face. "Kiss my...?"

"Hand," Ruga clarified, helpfully.

"But... Even if... This doesn't mean that we... I don't—"

But Ruga interrupted her by stepping away, still holding Elketh's hand around the fingers, her thumb keeping Elketh's palm open. "It was a yes or no question," she said. "If you don't answer properly, I'm going to assume 'no.' Make your decision."

Elketh's frantic gaze darted back to the guard. Was she looking for help, or because she didn't want to be witnessed? Ruga wondered. She wasn't held in suspense for long. Elketh's chest rose and fell at a quickened pace as she strangled out, "Yes."

Keeping her eyes on Elketh the entire time, Ruga pressed Elketh's fingertips to her lips. Elketh's throat bobbed as she swallowed. As Ruga made her way down Elketh's hand with her mouth, she felt the archery calluses, rubbing roughly against her lips in some areas, her skin silk-soft in others. Elketh's eyes became half-lidded, fluttering, as Ruga pushed an open-mouthed kiss into Elketh's palm.

Ruga couldn't help but smile into Elketh's hand right before she released it—it was almost as though she'd cast a spell. Dazed, Elketh held her hand up in the air for a few seconds more before promptly dropping it to her side.

"Will you need a bath drawn?" Ruga asked. She did not particularly feel like going back downstairs to cart up heated water. No one in the castle took as many baths as Elketh requested. Ruga was not entirely convinced that Elketh didn't ask for them just to inconvenience her.

"No," Elketh said. "I don't need one."

At the end of the hall, the guard cleared his throat. Elketh came away from the wall, swinging Ruga's bedchamber door open, and went inside.

They changed in silence, facing away from each other, even though there was hardly anything to see in the light of the room's singular flickering candle. It was a relief to Ruga to have her wardrobe back. She picked her silkiest shift to sleep in and climbed into bed as Elketh washed up. It wasn't long before Elketh blew the candle out.

"I suppose you want me to sleep on the floor," Elketh's disembodied voice said, which Ruga took as a sly way of Elketh inviting herself into bed via pity.

"Not at all," said Ruga.

"Then *you* can sleep on the floor," Elketh said.

"This is my bed. I have not slept here in weeks. You're welcome to join me, though. I've been told I excel at hospitality."

There was grumbling from the opposite side of the bed, and then the mattress dipped as Elketh settled in. Even without touching each other, the bed was warmer, and sleep pulled at Ruga's eyes.

The last thought Ruga had before she fell asleep was that she quite liked her bed with Elketh in it.

CHAPTER SEVENTEEN

There was a toned, scantily clad woman in bed next to Elketh, which meant Elketh's chances of a proper night of sleep were slim. To Elketh's frustration, Ruga had no such qualms. She was snoozing away, her breaths even. Ruga looked almost peaceful in sleep, the sharp line of her jaw softened by the dim light coming in through the window. Her lips appeared kissably plump. Actually, Elketh now *knew* they were as soft as they looked.

Elketh was staring. Huffing, she turned over, facing away from Ruga and toward the window, and closed her eyes as though that would help. Elketh couldn't help but think of Ruga in the hallway outside—confident, stable, quiet Ruga, pinning Elketh to the wall and demanding to know if she wanted to be kissed.

Behind closed eyes, Elketh saw Ruga gingerly taking her hand and touching her fingertips to her lips. More than that, Elketh felt the warmth of Ruga's mouth on the palm of her open hand, the dampness on the inside of Ruga's lips. The surprising graze of Ruga's tusks on either side of Elketh's palm, sharper than she thought they would be, a slight but somehow pleasant sting.

Lightly, Elketh touched the raised lines on her hand where Ruga's tusks had been—undeniable evidence that it had happened, that she hadn't just dreamed it.

She saw, too, the smug look on Ruga's face, like she knew exactly the effect she was having on Elketh and relished it.

It seemed unfair that Ruga had been the one making moon eyes at Elketh all day, but Elketh was the one kept awake.

Elketh didn't have to touch between her legs to know she was wet, though she greatly wanted to. If Ruga hadn't been there, she might have. She lay in discomfort instead, taking controlled breaths, trying to think chaste, placid thoughts.

She failed. Badly. Elketh imagined Ruga's mouth elsewhere on her body, pressing under her breasts, kissing lower and...

Cursing, Elketh turned back to face Ruga. "Ruga?" she whispered.

There was no response.

"Ruga?" she tried again.

Instantly, Ruga's breathing became lighter. Elketh hardly dared to move. She wasn't sure if she wanted Ruga to wake or not. Ruga was on her back, the blanket tangled around her torso. Her nipples were hard through the fabric of her shift. Unbidden, saliva filled Elketh's mouth.

She crept closer to Ruga. The bed dipped noticeably, and Ruga slid a bit towards her. Ruga grunted, throwing an arm over her stomach.

This was it. Elketh laid a hand over Ruga's, giving herself a second to feel the corded muscle in Ruga's forearm. "Ruga," Elketh said again, softly, and Ruga's eyes snapped open.

"Elketh?" Ruga asked. She rubbed at her eye with her knuckles. "What is it?"

Hastily, Elketh retracted her hand. "Nothing."

"You woke me up for nothing," Ruga repeated, to clarify. She sat herself up on her elbows. "Did you have a bad dream?"

"I can handle bad dreams," Elketh snapped.

"I'm going back to sleep," Ruga said, and closed her eyes.

"Wait!"

Again, Ruga opened her eyes. She did not look very happy about it.

"I...was going to go into another room to take care of something," Elketh said, her mouth unbearably dry, "but I thought I would give you the chance to take care of it first."

Ruga rolled to face Elketh. They were very close. Elketh forced herself to look Ruga in the eye. "Are you serious?" Ruga asked, toneless.

"Maybe I wasn't clear."

The mirth on Ruga's face made it apparent that Elketh's intent had come through. "One palm kiss, and now this? Don't you think it's a bit fast?"

She was certainly teasing, but Elketh couldn't tell if Ruga was kidding, too. "Yes?" Elketh tried.

Ruga glanced down and back up again. Elketh blushed furiously when she realized she was being checked out. "What do you want me to do?" Ruga asked.

Touch me, Elketh was sure she meant to say, but it came out as, "Kiss me," instead.

So Ruga set a hand against the back of Elketh's neck, her thumb on Elketh's throat, and brought her close, and kissed her. Ruga's lips were just as warm and pleasant as Elketh remembered—warmer, even—and Elketh opened her mouth to accept Ruga's tongue; she surprised herself with how much she liked it, kissing Ruga.

It was a slow, controlled kiss, like many things about Ruga were, and Elketh pushed for speed, clutching Ruga's wrist tightly, until they were frantic and entangled, Elketh's hair wrapped around Ruga's knuckles and Ruga's tusks pressing into the side of Elketh's jaw as she kissed there and the spot underneath, right where Elketh was sensitive.

Elketh gasped. Intuitively, Ruga pressed deeper into the spot. Elketh bunched her fist in the front of Ruga's shift, squirming. "Fuck," she breathed.

"Should I?" Ruga asked against Elketh's neck, still kissing it. Her warm breath raised goosebumps on Elketh's skin.

"Please."

"What do you like?" Ruga whispered right in Elketh's ear. Elketh shuddered.

"I hear from your librarian," Elketh said with effort, "that orcs have very talented tongues."

Ruga raised her eyebrows suggestively. She inched the thin sleeve of Elketh's shift down and kissed her shoulder.

This was not something Elketh did with people, she thought as Ruga's other hand slid up a thigh, lifting Elketh's shift above her navel, over her ribs, until it became tangled around Elketh's neck and she had to take it all the way off herself. Elketh did not engage in sex like this: affectionately intimate, mouths on places just to feel the skin there.

The way Ruga lay next to Elketh, doing nothing else but staring at Elketh's body like it was something lovely, made her feel naked—not just naked in the literal sense, but down to the bone, to the core of herself, and she could only watch Ruga's face for any hint that Ruga found something ugly there, something unworthy.

As if in answer to an unspoken question, Ruga cupped Elketh's hip and pulled her close for another kiss that started at her mouth and ended in a string of quick, soft pecks down the side of her neck, against her collarbone, the flat area right above her breast. The tusks grazed her skin, a contrasting sensation to the pillowy softness of the kisses. Ruga glanced up at Elketh as if asking for permission, and Elketh somehow had enough sense left to agree with a nod.

A warm hand brushed against Elketh's breast, and she couldn't help but let out a moan when Ruga put the other nipple in her mouth, swirling it with her tongue like a promise of things to come. Ruga lifted her head; Elketh's skin was cold in the sudden absence.

"Can I touch you?" Ruga asked, breathy.

"If you don't, I will," Elketh said, and it came out harsher than she meant it. "You're too damn polite."

If Ruga was offended by her tone, she didn't show it—she just laughed and lowered her mouth back to Elketh's nipple as her hand caressed the skin of Elketh's torso, the curve of her belly, into the mound of hair between her legs. The nipple was starting to get sore, and somehow that turned Elketh on more.

Ruga parted Elketh with two of her fingers and slid them down the wet length of her cunt. Elketh bit down her lip to stop from crying out. Her fist clenched around the sheets to stabilize herself as practiced fingers massaged her clit. And still, Ruga caressed the nipple with her tongue.

Elketh's other hand came around to hold Ruga's head down, slipping under the horns she'd been so skeptical of before. "Ruga...I...I'm close," Elketh gasped out.

Ruga shook Elketh's hand away as she lifted her head again, and then Elketh was being pushed up into the pillows as Ruga shifted lower on the bed. With one shoulder, Ruga nudged Elketh's leg so the knee was bent, her hand slowing. The talented fingers switched out with a quick tongue. Elketh bucked right away and orgasmed right on Ruga's face—against the flat part of Ruga's tongue, against her tusks and lips and chin.

"Fuck," Elketh said again, because the other words she knew had all left her.

Gently, Ruga continued to lap at Elketh's vulva after it was over. Elketh felt another orgasm building, a sensation that started where Ruga touched her and radiated all over her body, the tightening before release. She watched Ruga's purple head of hair bob up and down, wearing an almost peaceful expression, her long eyelashes lining the curve of her closed eyes.

Ruga reached up with one hand and squeezed the skin around Elketh's breast. Badly, Elketh wanted to grab onto Ruga's horns when she rode her face. She unclenched the sheets to touch one of Ruga's horns with tentative fingers; Ruga's other hand closed over hers, guiding Elketh to fold her knuckles over the horn. It was hard like wood, curving over the back of Ruga's skull.

Ruga pressed harder into Elketh's clit, her tongue picking up momentum. Elketh's grip tightened on the horn as her second orgasm came. She thrust her hips at Ruga's face, leaning into the burst of pleasure. Ruga fucked her with her mouth through it as Elketh held on for dear life, embarrassing little noises escaping her throat.

Elketh released Ruga and slumped back into the sheets, her body like elastic, sore and damp and absolutely, positively satisfied. On the other end of the bed, Ruga lifted herself to her knees. Sweaty hair stuck to her forehead and the sides of her face, but she had a certain brightness about her, a glow. "I thought you were going to rip my horn off," Ruga said with a dazed little smile.

"Sorry," Elketh murmured.

"Don't be." Ruga crawled back up to the top of the bed and settled herself against the pillows with a sigh. "How was it?"

Elketh swallowed. She hadn't had sex like that since she was younger, when the prospect of spending a millennium with one person sounded like the most romantic idea in the world. "I didn't feel any magic orc tongue tricks."

Ruga laughed that rough laugh of hers; Elketh really was starting to like it quite a bit. "I was saving it for next time," Ruga said, which made Elketh's stomach flop because she had not yet been thinking of a "next time" at all. She wasn't sure what it would mean if there was one.

"Did you enjoy yourself?" Elketh thought to ask when Ruga handed her her shift. She realized she hadn't seen Ruga without her clothes. It was hard to be too disappointed about that.

Ruga was up now, wiping her face with a cloth after having splashed it with water. "Immensely," she said, and her honesty embarrassed Elketh more than the act of waking up a jilted fiancée in the middle of the night just to seduce them.

Elketh left the bed to clean herself up as soon as Ruga came back, and she reentered the bedchamber to find Ruga sitting on the end of the bed, looking like she didn't intend to go back to sleep. "What?" Elketh asked. And then realized, because she was always forgetting her manners: "Did you need me to do you too? I'm a bit of a princess of the pillows, to be honest. But I can try."

"I guessed that," Ruga said, the corners of her eyes crinkling in amusement. "No, I'm fine." She was holding a tin of something pungent.

"The salve?" Elketh asked. She had forgotten about the blisters that plagued her all day. Apparently, orgasms were a great cure for pain.

"Come here," Ruga said.

Elketh stepped between Ruga's spread legs. She should sit down, she thought, but Ruga had salve on her finger and was rubbing it into a spot on Elketh's neck where Ruga's tusks had broken skin. The salve was cool against Elketh's overly warm skin, but she hated to ask Ruga to stop, to admit that she kind of liked the sting, the reminder.

Ruga rubbed the salve into every angry line her tusks left behind and then had Elketh sit on the bed so she could do the same for her feet.

"Thank you," Elketh said.

"Should we go to sleep?" The tin popped close with a metallic click.

"We should."

They settled back under the covers. The air was different now—not quite charged but loaded with implications, the musk of sex lingering heavily. Elketh closed her eyes. It wasn't weird, she reminded herself. She did this all the time with other people. It didn't change anything about her situation here.

Why did it feel so different to do it with Ruga, then?

At her side, Ruga was already falling back asleep. Elketh wished she could be like that, unbothered by thoughts and feelings. Now that Elketh knew how warm Ruga was, inside and out, she was overcome with an urge to get closer. Conscious of her movements, so as not to wake Ruga, she nudged closer little by little, until she was flush against Ruga's side.

"All good?" Ruga asked sleepily.

Stars. "Yes, I—"

"Wanted to cuddle," Ruga finished for her, cutting her off. She turned onto her side. "Go ahead."

"That's not the word I was going to use," Elketh protested weakly. But she put an arm over Ruga and nuzzled into her warm back, burying her face in that comfortable, earthy smell.

"Good night, Elketh."

Elketh murmured something into Ruga's back.

"What was that?" Ruga asked.

"That was nice. It was just...very nice."

Ruga lifted Elketh's hand to her mouth and kissed it.

CHAPTER EIGHTEEN

Ruga woke to the sun high in the sky with an elf wrapped around her.

Her bladder pressed at her urgently, but she was too comfortable to get up, and she didn't want to wake Elketh—didn't want to break the spell that was whatever had happened in the middle of the night. If not for Elketh's embrace and the lingering taste of her on Ruga's tongue, Ruga would have thought last night only happened in her imagination.

When she couldn't stand her bladder anymore, Ruga rolled Elketh off of her to relieve herself. The destroyed crown already felt like it had happened to someone else in another lifetime. She almost allowed herself to forget the impending consequences when Freya figured out what Ruga had covered up.

She returned to bed, where Elketh blinked up at her, hair charmingly askew, the covers pulled up to her chin.

"You seduced me," Elketh accused.

"I seduced *you?*" Ruga asked. "Elketh, you woke me up so I could go down on you."

"I wouldn't have if you hadn't kissed my hand like that."

Ruga sat down on the side of the bed. It was a fear of hers that Elketh would react poorly in the morning. She'd have given all the coin in the treasury to know what Elketh was thinking. "Do you regret it?" she asked finally.

"No," came the answer right away.

Tentatively, Ruga placed her hand on Elketh's shoulder. "Are you upset with how much you like being here, even though you didn't want to come?"

"No. I think I'm upset with..."

Hardening her heart against something sharp, Ruga waited. The elf had never wanted to be in Torden. Even with all the drama Elketh had caused, Ruga kept forgetting that.

"I'm upset with how much I like *you*."

The shields around Ruga's heart crumbled. "Really?" she asked.

Elketh sat up. The blanket slid down, reminding Ruga of why she had not minded being woken up very much. "Yes, really. I—I mean, I'm not going to marry you for the alliance thing."

"I know that," Ruga said.

"But you've made it nice to be here."

"I'm really glad you feel that way, Elketh." Ruga blinked rapidly so that the wetness lining her eyes was less obvious.

But Elketh never paid as little attention as she pretended to. "Oh, come here, you sap," Elketh said, and took hold of the sides of Ruga's face to kiss her.

The sex was somehow sweeter in the light of day—not secretive like it had been at night, where it could have been a dream or a plausibly deniable mistake. Elketh's skin was warm from sleep and the sun. Ruga crawled back under the covers, cradling Elketh's head as they kissed, her heart rate accelerating.

She gasped when Elketh raised her knee into Ruga's shift and rubbed her shin between Ruga's legs.

Elketh moaned when Ruga returned the favor. It was a gratifying sound, something Ruga wished she could capture, frozen in time, and return to again and again. Slowly, they rubbed against each other, mouths still connected, skin to skin, like they were taking extra time to appreciate the buildup.

Ruga almost liked the slick sensation of Elketh rubbing against her thigh more than the feeling of her own pussy on Elketh's leg. She liked it even more when Elketh tensed against her and moaned into her mouth, holding onto the back of Ruga's neck like a lifeline, and then slumped back into the sheets.

Ruga allowed herself one last kiss before she slid down next to Elketh. The elf glanced over at her with those pretty brown eyes.

"I like you, too, for the record," Ruga said.

"I could tell," Elketh said with a laugh. "That's why I woke you up."

And Ruga tried to suppress it a bit, because it couldn't last, but a warm glow kindled in her chest. She knew it would be hard to put out.

Laughter came from the window, accompanied by a loud, festive bang and cheers. Today was the first day of the midsummer festival; the main festivities took place in the town square. The early birds would already be starting, and Ruga was most certainly expected to attend. She had also most certainly missed the entirety of breakfast.

Elketh crept to the window, a breeze jostling her shift. "What's going on?"

"The solstice." It occurred to Ruga that the Elven Islands might not celebrate. "We have celebrations all day. You'll be expected to come, too, if it's not too much trouble. I can find us some clothes."

Elketh winced. "What kind of celebrations, exactly?"

Ruga was already at the wardrobe, filtering through her own dresses and the ones the seamstress had delivered for Elketh. The theme was summer colors, lush greens like the rolling hills or warm oranges like the setting sun. She selected one for herself and one for Elketh as she explained. "Lots of things. Food, dancing, drinking, games. General revelry. It's time off for almost everyone, except in the castle. Our kitchens work overtime to put out more than enough food for the town. People come from all over to visit." She set Elketh's dress on the sheets. "There's a celebration in every major city. I think ours is the best, though."

"Wow," Elketh said. "In Branwen, we spend three days in temple on our knees praying to the goddess. It's very austere. I guess I'm lucky to be here for it this year."

"That's surprising," Ruga said. She had thought she had some kind of rudimentary knowledge of elvish customs. "I thought your people liked revelry."

"And I thought your people were warlike and uncultured," Elketh said. "I guess we both defy expectations."

That was an understatement if Ruga had ever heard one. "Will you come?" she asked.

"I already did."

It took Ruga a moment; she snorted.

"Yes, I'll go to the celebration. It sounds like a good time."

"It is," Ruga said, beaming. She donned her dress, swishing it around in the mirror to make sure it wasn't wrinkled. The dress was yellow, not too baggy so she could dance properly, hemmed with floral decorations at the neckline and sleeves. "The festival is one of my favorite events of the year. There will be skalds reciting tales, wrestlers to watch, folks dancing in a line, children running around—all of the things that make life worth living. I always look forward to it. And it's six days long, not three."

"Six whole days of fun? That's hedonistic." Elketh appeared behind Ruga in the mirror. Her slender fingers picked at the lace of Ruga's dress. In her reflection, Elketh smiled with the corner of her mouth like she was hiding something.

"What has you so giddy?" Ruga asked. It made sense that Elketh would be excited. She was the kind of person to appreciate indulgence.

"Nothing," Elketh said. "You just look happy. It's contagious." She tied off the top of Ruga's dress and then turned for Ruga to help her with her own. As Ruga was lacing, Elketh turned around and pressed a gentle kiss to the side of Ruga's cheek. "I'm still waiting to experience that tongue trick."

"You will, next time," Ruga promised. She felt the smile Elketh gave her down to her toes.

Strangers filed onto the castle grounds, helping themselves to the elaborate tables of food set out by the kitchen staff in the great hall. Many people wouldn't stay there to eat so they could see the wrestlers setting up in the town square. There would be an increased guard presence today for Queen Astrid with every available body on duty, but to do something against the queen on this holy day would be considered almost sacrilegious, an affront to the goddess herself.

The concern, of course, was not from within Torden.

Ruga wrapped honey-roasted nuts in paper as Elketh ladled onion porridge into a portable cone. They ate as they walked. Children filtered around them, shrieking in delight, their fingers sticky with honey and stained with chalk. There were chalk drawings everywhere on the road leading away from the castle—signposts and trees alike were at high risk of being doodled on, and the sides of buildings stretched with colorful, if not artfully done, images of flowers and stick figures with horns.

"I'm trying to remember everything so I can change Branwen's solstice customs when I get back," Elketh said. "I never want to spend another day in the temple again."

"We should go to temple, actually," Ruga said. "My sister will be there."

Elketh wrinkled her nose, but she followed Ruga on the path up the hill to the temple, separate from the rest of the town. The temple was full when they got there, so full people loitered outside, chatting and sharing stories. A giant pile of pottery shards and little sculptures squared the tall, open main room on each side—symbolic sacrifices. A priestess stood at the plain stone altar, projecting her voice, but Elketh's tense shoulders slumped back down when she saw it all.

"It's not as formal as I thought it would be," Elketh said. Behind the priestess, the queen sat in a simple chair with her lady's maid, Freya, standing behind her—they were about the same height, the human standing and the orc sitting. To their right was a large statue of the goddess holding her hands up to bless the people.

"The goddess in your temple is an orc."

"Of course she is," Ruga said. "What else would she be?"

"Our temples have an elf goddess."

An elf goddess was the most preposterous thing Ruga had ever heard of, but because it was apparent Elketh felt the same way about the orc goddess, Ruga kept her mouth shut. As soon as the sermon ended, people rushed down the hill, brushing past the group coming for the next sermon. Unlike everyone else, Queen Astrid, her lady's maid, and the priestesses would be in the temple nearly all day until the final feast. Ruga did not envy them.

In an endless stream of delicious food, Ruga and Elketh snacked, accepting sweetmeats on sticks in the shape of the goddess passed around on the street. Though Ruga was used to the sights and loved them, she especially enjoyed Elketh's reactions to the goings around. Ruga gave her coin to throw at a busker wearing down his lyre as Elketh swayed subconsciously to the music.

The acrobat troupe, in from Sydlig in the south, was spectacular, juggling flaming batons and passing them back and forth to each other, and dressed in very little. Ruga watched Elketh take in their toned forms—she was learning that Elketh was big on buff women—and their lithe movements, orange light flickering off of their faces. Other tricks of theirs were even more magnificent as they tightrope walked between buildings and swung against each other in impressive stunts.

"You should pick up that hobby," Elketh said, unable to look away.

There were barrels of ale and mead, and people passed around drinking horns to dunk into them. Several orcs had taken it upon themselves to engage in drinking contests, though they were officially discouraged. Elketh cheered the loudest as an orc woman, nearly seven feet tall, beat out one of Torden's soldiers. Someone handed them three-dimensional models of stars on sticks made by children. Joyfully, they waved them in circles, twirling them in the wind.

Ruga slid her hand into Elketh's like it was the most natural thing in the world, and Elketh let her.

A little buzzed on mead and ale, they sat down to dinner at the end of the day as a priestess put on a fireworks display, her staff waving around to control the illusion. The tables were set out in the middle of the town square surrounding the gurgling fountain. Earlier today, the tables and food had been painstakingly brought down here by surplus hired hands, and now, people Ruga knew and people she'd never met sat down to dine together. It was the one time of the year since the Lynby nonsense that Ruga truly felt the orc countries could live harmoniously.

The weather was beautiful even after the sun set. The space by the town square was lit by magic lights that children got up to chase around, parents following in gleeful disarray. Queen Astrid and her guard dined at their own table, separate enough to discourage anyone from coming near them, which allowed Ruga and Elketh to be more anonymous with the masses. Ruga wasn't particularly hungry after filling her belly all day, but she picked at pastries drizzled with honey.

"You have a sweet tooth, don't you?" Elketh asked as she watched Ruga eat. Her eyes were a little watery with drink.

Ruga tried to hide how pleased she was that Elketh had observed her enough to pick up on that. "I do, yes."

"I'll have to keep that in mind for when I want to treat you."

The glow in Ruga's chest expanded, burning brightly.

Everyone turned when the queen rose from her table, silence overtaking the boisterous chatter. Queen Astrid gave her people a rare smile. "Thank you, everyone, for coming today to the solstice celebration. I hope that this has been a pleasant time of togetherness. Maybe a few of you have spared a thought for the goddess, as well," she said good-humoredly, which elicited several laughs and rounds of cheer. "So long as we share the same skies with the same stars, everyone is welcome in Torden. When our souls are reincarnated, we will be together like this once more, united by wyrd in our love for our people."

She took her seat again, never one to share overlong speeches. This one was a summary of a customary speech passed down for generations.

Several musicians took their places from a brightly painted caravan in the middle of the square, one of them sitting on the lip of the central fountain with a lyre.

"What now?" Elketh asked as the chatter started back up again.

"Dancing," Ruga said.

"No one is getting up to dance," Elketh pointed out. It was true. No one stepped in when the instruments started up. The traveling skald stood in the middle of them, melodiously reciting a tale to an upbeat tune.

"Tradition dictates," said Ruga, "that the first person to dance has to do it completely alone, and everyone has to watch. This song is meant to be danced solo."

Elketh's eyes twinkled with mischief. "I dare you to be the first."

Ruga hoped Elketh would say that. "I accept your challenge."

CHAPTER NINETEEN

When Elketh dared Ruga to dance, she had not thought Ruga would actually do it, but Ruga jumped up to the encouraging stamping of feet around her. It was apparent when Ruga took her place in the center of the square, looking around to make sure that people were watching, that she actually quite liked it. Elketh didn't think of Ruga as someone who yearned for attention—not the way Elketh did—but she was finding Ruga was very intentional about when the focus was on her. Similar to Elketh, Ruga seemed to thrive under it.

Ruga began to dance. It was a folk-type jig, a joyous thing that involved a lot of twirling and kicking. While Ruga was not a particularly graceful or limber dancer, each movement was controlled and deliberate, much like Ruga herself. Elketh had her eyes glued on Ruga to the end, the broad grin on her face, the playful nature with which Ruga approached tables to pirouette for the people there to raucous cheering. Her dress caught the light, the golden thread of its decorations reflecting the magic lights fluttering around the square.

She was stunning.

By the end of the performance, a swarm of people had gotten up to dance to the next song, and Ruga returned to Elketh, a bit sweaty and breathless.

"Come on," Ruga said, exhilarated, holding out her hand palm-up.

It took Elketh a moment to understand what she wanted. "Oh, I don't know any orcish dances." What a bummer, too, because it looked like everyone else was having so much fun. They had almost all paired up, some of them even in threes, and now they swung each other around to the newest upbeat tune.

"I can lead," Ruga said.

A thrill coursed through Elketh as she took Ruga's outstretched hand.

People pushed the tables back to clear extra space around the fountain. Ruga started Elketh out slower than everyone else, showing her the prance-like move the others were doing as she counted out the beat. "Okay, okay, I know enough to do that," Elketh said, laughing, and Ruga brought her up to speed.

Hand-in-hand, they sashayed back and forth, switching directions on cue from the music and the masses around them. Ruga grinned the whole time.

Her joy was infectious.

The dance ended in a long, snaking line of people looping around together, Elketh's left hand in Ruga's and her right in a stranger's. The music grew to a crescendo, the skald fighting to be heard above it all.

Far too soon, it was over. Pairs separated from the line once again for the next dance.

Ruga pulled Elketh to the side—not completely out of the square, still among the dancers, but she made no motion to show Elketh the next set of moves. "Elketh," Ruga said, and Elketh shut her eyes in unbridled happiness at the sound of her own name. "Elketh, I really want to kiss you where everyone can see us. Is that okay?"

Elketh's eyes snapped open. It wasn't really a secret, was it, that they were getting along well? And the only bad thing that could happen was that Elketh would leave the orcs behind on this note of false hope, kept secret by a select few in the queen's close circle—something they would have to deal with by the end of their engagement period. Maybe it wasn't a good idea, she thought. Maybe it was something they needed to think through more.

And then Elketh looked up into Ruga's face and knew she couldn't say no to her.

The kiss was gentle and sweet. Elketh couldn't help but think about the things that made up Ruga: the softness of her lips and the sharp bite of her tusks, the gentleness of her soul and the rough edges of her figure, the quietness of her voice and her powerful influence over Vakker.

Ruga was a bundle of harmonious contradictions. A paradox Elketh wanted the time to get to know better.

Elketh melted into Ruga like liquid, her arms around Ruga's neck in the middle of all the dancers. One of the dancers bumped into them, breaking off the kiss. They just looked at each other, both giddy. It had been a long time since Elketh had felt this way about anyone.

Someone jostled them again. Two firm hands reached between the couple and pried them apart. Elketh fumbled backward, ready to give the interloper a piece of her mind, and locked eyes with a guard in leather armor.

Hedda, her features twisted in anger.

Elketh backed away, just barely missing Hedda's outstretched hand as she grabbed for Elketh's dress.

"Hedda, stop!" Ruga shouted. People around them scrambled away; the music continued despite the chaos. "What are you doing?"

"It's not fair," Hedda said, slurring, and only then did Elketh realize how inebriated the guard was. "*We're* supposed to be dancing."

As far as Elketh was concerned, Hedda could dance with Ruga, too. The guards were on-duty, but she'd seen them in the crowds, participating in the fun. Hadn't Hedda also danced with plenty of strangers tonight already?

"Hedda, please don't do this," Ruga said, her voice low.

"You've moved on quick," Hedda said bitterly. "Never cared for *me*. Never cared."

Two guards came running from Queen Astrid's table, pushing people aside to hold Hedda back. "Queen Astrid wants to speak with you," one of them said. "Come on, Hedda."

"Fuck the queen," Hedda said, swaying with drunkenness. The guards and Ruga collectively inhaled gasps. "Why should she determine my wyrd?"

"You swore to serve her," the other guard reminded Hedda.

"Didn't swear to give up love for her."

"*Hedda*," Ruga warned.

"No, you—you shut up! Why don't you keep smacking lips with this spoiled elf? She seems to like it." The guards exchanged a look behind Hedda and both tightened their grip on her shoulders. "You're sleeping with her, aren't you?"

Something registered in Elketh's mind, something she maybe knew subconsciously. Pieces began to fall into place: Hedda's anger at Elketh, the insistence on sharing Elketh's destruction of the crown with Ruga instead of the queen.

The two guards hauled Hedda away. The music sputtered and then started up even louder. Elketh glanced over at the musicians. The queen's maid was whispering to them, giving them what looked like an urgent message to keep up the music at all costs. It seemed to be working. Everyone was back to dancing, and Hedda was already so far away that no one could hear her yelling.

"I am so sorry about that," Ruga said. She was nearly in tears.

"You dated Hedda?" Elketh cried above the music.

Ruga nodded.

"The queen had you break it off with her," Elketh shouted. "For the arrangement with Branwen. With me."

"Yes, Elketh."

"And you're... How long ago, exactly, was that?"

Ruga said something Elketh couldn't hear over a sudden whoop of the audience. They were switching partners now. Someone tried to grab hold of Elketh's arm to bring her into the loop. Roughly, she shook them off.

"What?"

"Six months or so."

Elketh broke away from the dancers in the town square and headed back up the trail to the castle. Damn it. Six *months*? And Elketh had known for less than a day before the arrangement was foisted upon her, known only as long as it took that ferry to cross the channel between Branwen and Torden.

She wanted to smash something. Preferably her father's face. If only she wasn't completely convinced he would dump her in the sea if she tried to row herself back to Branwen's sandy shores.

She didn't lose her pace when she heard Ruga running after her, and she didn't slow down even as she stomped up the small set of stairs that led to the rose garden, her feet aching with each heavy step.

Ruga caught up to her at the gated arch outside the garden, reaching for her hand. Nearly out of breath, Elketh turned to her, anger coursing through her entire body.

"Elketh, you knew..." Ruga stopped to catch her breath. "You knew that I agreed to the betrothal in advance. I'm sorry. I would have told you sooner if I thought it was important."

Elketh covered her face with her free hand. It wasn't Ruga's fault. There was no need to take her feelings out on Ruga.

"I'm not upset with *you*," Elketh managed to say, as nice as she could make it sound. "I just...need a minute alone, all right?"

"All right," Ruga said, and let go of Elketh's hand. Elketh eased the gate behind her, even though she wanted to slam it, and slumped to the ground.

It's not fair, Hedda had said. On that count, she'd been right. Elketh fumed. She was a woman often made up of ugly emotions, something that never seemed so true as it was now.

Elketh knew herself enough to recognize this ugliness for what it was: jealousy.

She was jealous of what Ruga and Hedda had, what they'd had up until six months ago. The organic nature of it. They'd chosen each other; they hadn't been forced together. She was envious of Ruga's situation, that she had so much time to prepare herself mentally for the engagement when Elketh had none.

How long had Ruga and Hedda known each other? Hundreds of years, maybe their whole lives. And how long had Elketh known Ruga? Less than three whole weeks. How presumptuous Elketh had been to think that she may be important to Ruga when Ruga had this whole history with Hedda that Elketh had not known of. They had clearly loved each other.

Hedda wouldn't have acted out like that unless she loved Ruga.

Accentuated by light from the festivities below, Ruga's shadow towered past the entrance to the gardens. Elketh got her breathing under control and opened the gate.

"How long were you together?" Elketh asked without preamble.

Gently, Ruga closed the gate. Her eyes were rimmed red. "Twenty years. This would have been our twenty-first. We first got together at the summer solstice," she said, nearly choking on her words.

"And the queen forced you to end your relationship?" Elketh demanded.

"She asked me if I would. Your father, the king, he reached out to Astrid and offered a marriage alliance. She suggested an earl first, but he said his daughter was worth a princess." Ruga kept her eyes skyward. "I broke off the relationship with Hedda. By choice. For Torden and its people."

Elketh was angrier at her father than ever. "You loved her."

"Of course I did, Elketh," Ruga said, her voice breaking on Elketh's name. A tear dropped down the curve of her cheek. "Of course I did."

"Do you still?" Elketh asked, intertwining and disentangling her fingers with nerves.

Ruga's breathing was labored, shaky. "I don't."

An unasked question died on Elketh's lips. She didn't need to be shot down by asking it. Not without knowing herself how she would answer such a question directed at her.

Elketh wagered that Hedda had been a good lover. Someone willing to duel for Ruga's honor in literal combat, perhaps the reason Hedda was in that line of service. Elketh wasn't like that. She'd never fought on anyone's behalf but her own. That was what had driven her to stupidity when she destroyed the ceremonial crown that meant so much to the orcs and nothing to her. Now that Hedda was mad, it was only a matter of time before she told someone important about what Elketh had done. It seemed too late to change now. To be the kind of person worthy of Ruga's affections.

"Stars," Elketh swore, lowering herself onto the stone bench in the garden. "I'm so sorry, Ruga. I'm sorry that my father tricked you into breaking off an important connection for someone who doesn't want to marry you." She sniffled. "Branwen wouldn't have deserved you, you know. Anyone who is dutiful enough to sever a meaningful romantic relationship for their country shouldn't be subjected to this. You got your heart broken for no reason."

Wordlessly, Ruga knelt at Elketh's feet. She placed her head in Elketh's lap. With trembling fingers, Elketh stroked Ruga's soft hair, her horns.

"I hope you know that you can be with Hedda if you want," Elketh said. "We never should've started...this." She didn't have a good word for it. Sharing a bed didn't encapsulate the complexity of Elketh's feelings for Ruga.

"I don't regret it," Ruga said, muffled by the fabric of Elketh's dress. "I would do it again."

Ruga lifted her head, leaning into Elketh's hand as Elketh trailed fingers over her horns.

"You're not just saying that?" Elketh asked.

Ruga pressed a kiss to Elketh's wet cheek. "I want to be with you," Ruga said. She cupped Elketh's face, running a thumb over the next tear to fall.

Elketh's heart roared at her, spurring her to action. "Stand up," she ordered.

Ruga did.

Elketh eased herself off of the bench and bent down in the grass where Ruga had slept to make Elketh comfortable.

"Disrobe."

Ruga did. The pretty golden-yellow dress that caught everyone's attention just an hour ago pooled at her feet.

Underneath her clothes, Ruga was even more beautiful than Elketh imagined. Moonlight caught on the edges of her defined muscles, biceps and abs in full contrast of light and deep shadow. Ruga's silky purple hair nearly reached her navel.

It may not have been in the temple, but Elketh was going to spend time on her knees today after all. *I will be worthy of you*, Elketh thought.

She shifted closer, one hand stretching up to caress the dip behind Ruga's hip, the curve of her ass, the firmness of a thigh. "Is this all right?" Elketh asked.

"Who's being too polite, now?" Ruga countered, eyes twinkling.

Elketh smiled. She reached a hand between Ruga's legs, parting her open, fingers touching through layers like the petals of the roses Ruga grew in her garden.

CHAPTER TWENTY

Ruga held herself still as Elketh touched her with slender fingers, starting out near Ruga's clit and then leaning in to taste Ruga with her mouth. Ruga's thighs clenched as Elketh entered her with two fingers; her tongue swirled around Ruga's clitoris.

So much for being a princess of the pillows, Ruga thought, rolling her head back as the orgasm built up against Elketh's busy mouth. Ruga grasped at Elketh's hair, grazing a feather-soft ear, as she came.

"Stars," Ruga whispered, lowering herself to Elketh's level to kiss her. Elketh's tongue flicked into Ruga's mouth, pressing into her, closer and closer. Ruga could taste herself on Elketh.

"I've had lots of practice," Elketh said. Ruga didn't miss that the elf took her sweet time touching Ruga's back muscles. "You taste damn good, Ruga."

Ruga nuzzled the side of Elketh's face. "I bet you say that to all your lays," she said playfully, to which Elketh laughed, a little breathless. "Turn around."

"Should I take off my—"

"No."

One inquisitive eyebrow raised, Elketh turned around, still on her knees. Gingerly, Ruga guided Elketh to flatten her back, bent over the bench, elbows supporting her against the stone.

"Am I going to find out about the tongue trick?" Elketh asked, wiggling her butt.

"Not if you keep talking."

Elketh stopped talking.

Ruga gripped the hem of Elketh's dress and nudged it over Elketh's knees, rolling it past her waist. She tugged down the bottom half of Elketh's smallclothes and kissed the bare skin of her lower back.

With one finger, Ruga reached between Elketh's legs to touch her. Elketh was wet—so incredibly wet. Turned on by turning Ruga on. It brought Ruga a special kind of pleasure to have such an obvious effect on her, to have Elketh spread open for her to do as she wished. This was the part Ruga liked most about sex. The trust, the vulnerability. And what a special treat it was for someone like Elketh to be vulnerable just for her.

Elketh shifted her hips as Ruga continued to touch her, skirts hiked up.

Ruga brought her face close; her tongue brushed against Elketh's cunt. A muffled moan echoed around the roses. As Ruga swept her middle finger over Elketh's clit, she entered Elketh with her tongue, quickly in and slowly out, a rhythm that brought Elketh to delicious little yelps. Ruga fucked Elketh with her tongue, faster and faster, until Elketh burst wetly over Ruga's face, dripping into Ruga's mouth and hand.

Ruga leaned backward, rolling back her tongue, and wiped her face against the hem of Elketh's dress. Elketh panted heavily.

"Penetrative tongue," Elketh murmured, almost dreamily. She was still slumped over the bench. "It's long."

"Plenty more where that came from," Ruga said. She settled down in the grass, just how she used to when she slept there. It wasn't long before Elketh joined her, curling up into Ruga's side. It was so natural, so easy for Ruga to put an arm over Elketh's waist to hold her close. Like they'd been doing it forever.

There had to be a way to convince Elketh to stay. Or to go through with the marriage alliance, at least. Ruga thought she wouldn't mind the Elven Islands so much, with Elketh there at her side. There had been a moment earlier when she thought Elketh was going to call it quits over the Hedda argument. Losing Elketh was a terrible concept, one Ruga hadn't had enough time to process until it was right there in front of her.

Ruga squeezed Elketh closer to her. The sounds of their steady breathing filled the air, the lingering noise of music floating up the hill to them. Ruga thought she could stay like this until the end of time.

Elketh broke the silence first. "You should probably call on whatever serv—staff member you have draw baths for me. I think I'm in need of one."

"Elketh," Ruga said, "*I've* been the one drawing baths for you."

"You're joking." Elketh lifted herself to look at Ruga. "You were carting all that water up the stairs this whole time?"

"There's a ramp for it," Ruga said. "As I told you before, we draw our own baths."

"I thought you were joking then, too."

"Go ahead on up," Ruga said. "I'll bring the water."

Elketh kissed Ruga's forehead before she got up to leave. "I'll see you in bed?"

"Of course," Ruga said, like a vow.

There was a soft whistling noise as Ruga slid back into her dress. Ruga had thought to gather a few minutes alone in her garden, but there was no such thing as alone time in a castle shared with Freya Wedd.

Freya was perched just outside the garden gate on a squat platform that, Ruga was sure, very recently contained a potted plant. Never far away, her falcon circled the sky above.

"What are you doing here?" Ruga asked.

"Easy," Freya chided. As usual, she was dressed in nondescript, dark clothing; hunched over, she looked even smaller than her five feet. Freya lifted an apple from some unknown place on her person and rubbed it against her tunic before taking a crunchy bite. The only apples available this time of year were bitter, tart things. "Are those wedding bells I hear?"

"Are you a voyeur now? Trying to catch people mid-copulation?"

Freya grinned at Ruga through a mouthful of apple. "Don't be too flattered. You're hardly the only person whose proclivities I track."

Ruga didn't doubt it. Very little slipped past Freya's watchful eyes.

"So?" Freya prompted.

"No," Ruga said. "She's opposed to it. Though I'm hoping to change her mind."

Freya looked up—a long way up—at Ruga from under her dark lashes. "You like her."

"Was I meant to hide my feelings?"

"Not necessarily." Apple juice dripped down Freya's chin at the next bite. Ruga had a flash of Elketh bent over the garden bench. "But it would be good if Elketh could honor our contract."

"I can't force her to do that."

Appraisingly, Freya nodded. "Seems like she likes you, too."

Not enough to turn her life around, Ruga thought. Not yet, anyway. "Don't get Astrid's hopes up."

"She saw the thing with Hedda."

"Who didn't?" Ruga asked evenly.

"Sorry about that," Freya said, as though Ruga hadn't spoken at all. "I misjudged Hedda's resentment. She was stealing drinks from other people. I didn't notice in time."

"She's a grown orc. You don't have to monitor her drinking."

"Apparently, I do," Freya said, cocking her head. "I am going to tell Astrid you're sleeping with the elf."

Suddenly exhausted, Ruga rubbed at her temples. "Whatever you like."

"Hedda won't be a problem," Freya said. "I spoke with her."

"Who all knows?" She didn't need to clarify that she meant the elf king's deception.

Freya ticked the people off on her fingers. "Astrid, Hedda, me. You. The librarian. Some of the félag, though they're sworn to secrecy, of course."

"Is there news from King Gareth? What's the plan if Elketh still doesn't want to marry me?"

"We have something," Freya said. "The queen wants to touch base with you in a week."

It seemed like Ruga's sister had less and less time for her lately. Even knowing Astrid had a plethora of queenly duties, it still stung.

Ruga closed her eyes, wrapped up the whiplash of her feelings, and put them to rest.

CHAPTER TWENTY-ONE

Elketh and Ruga began every morning with the communal breakfast in the great hall outside Vakker Castle, when they could be bothered to peel their sweaty post-rigor bodies out of bed. Notably, Hedda no longer dined with them at the queen's side. She'd been replaced with another soldier, and they were joined by the steward, who Elketh was informed usually woke up and dined so early people rarely saw him until he was ready to demand arrangements of you.

The second day of the festival, Ruga took Elketh to the next port town over so Elketh could try a spiced fish they were known for. There were even more fishmongers there than at Torden's harbor. The day after that, Elketh accompanied Ruga to the beach, where they splayed out in the sand; it made Elketh homesick for the beaches that bordered Branwen. Then, there were traders visiting, and a lively market ensued.

Once, when Elketh was running late for breakfast after deliberating too long over what dress to wear, she passed Hedda scrubbing the floors of the second-floor hallway. Hedda had sent a glare sharp and deadly as an axe Elketh's way. Elketh had never moved so fast in her life as she had to get away from Hedda then.

Middays were jam-packed with activities as Ruga shared her favorite places, things, and foods with Elketh. And then, at the end of the day, they sat down to the festival feast or sometimes skipped it so they could relax at the blacksmith forge, Ruga working on her chainmail and Elketh keeping her company.

It was a lovely, pleasurable time. Even when they did nothing, Elketh enjoyed Ruga's presence. Elketh had to concede that the orcs of Torden knew how to live. When Elketh planned a day of leisure back home, she had to abandon her father's imposed duties to do so. Here, devoting time to leisure was a norm. Expected. Elketh had never experienced anything like it in her life, and she deeply wanted more.

Before Elketh knew it, the festival was over, and it was once more Ruga's day to do rounds with the town complainers. The queen's handmaiden gave Ruga the list of people to check up on, which spiked Elketh's suspicion—what would a handmaiden know of the townspeople's mundane squabbles?

Elketh minded doing the rounds this time even less. The orcs who had poked and prodded her last time seemed to have gotten their fill, and they greeted her like an old friend now. It was easier to be polite to them, too, having danced with several of them at the solstice and shared meals.

Ruga explained that, once a month, they had an assembly where people could discuss issues the community faced and brainstorm solutions, which they then presented to the steward, who brought them to the queen—and then change was implemented, just like that. This, too, was strange to Elketh, whose father always had the final word when it came to changes (which he rarely implemented in the first place). Elketh had missed the last assembly when she was sulking in Ruga's rooms. She was very curious to know what it would look like.

Looming over Elketh, always, was the passage of time. It was not something she fretted over often. She had much of her life ahead of her, centuries to do all the things she wanted. Elketh had stopped physically tallying the days, counting down to the fiftieth when she could return home, but she kept track in her head without meaning to—and the day they did the rounds with the townspeople, they hit the halfway mark. Twenty-five days down, twenty-five to go.

She knew she had to assert to Ruga that, as well as they were getting along, she would be returning to Branwen alone once the betrothal period ended.

There were times, looking at Ruga, when Elketh wondered if it would be so bad to marry her and rule Branwen together. Whenever she thought this, a number of excuses popped up instantly: it wasn't fair to Ruga to sever her from Torden, a place she clearly loved; the six to eight hundred years or so left in their lifespans was plenty of time to be sick of each other, shackles instead of partnership; she wouldn't get to mess around with the Islands' population of lady elves anymore. Or maybe she could, but she would have to discuss it with Ruga first.

It was hard to deny that Elketh's connection to Ruga was significantly more emotionally fulfilling than those flings, though. And it wasn't like Ruga was failing her on the front of sexual needs. Being around Ruga was all positives and no negatives. Elketh felt her sharp edges soften around Ruga. She liked the person she was in Ruga's presence. Through Ruga's eyes. Most often, she worried that Ruga was far too good for her—that while Elketh's life was enriched by Ruga, Ruga's life was worse with Elketh in it.

So her inner debate went, back and forth, some days entirely convinced that she could easily spend the rest of her years with Ruga, some days so opposed that it seemed like the worst idea she'd ever had.

The few weeks left to them were hardly enough time for Elketh to decide. More often, she swayed toward leaving Ruga behind and falling back into her old ways. It would be a disservice to both of them if Elketh brought Ruga with her to Branwen and changed her mind after.

Elketh considered telling Ruga that she intended to leave as Ruga had her bent over the bench in the garden. She considered telling her when Ruga had her up against the wall in an alleyway. She even considered telling her when Ruga took her hand with so much affection that Elketh could feel her own heart melt. And each time, cowardice kept her from bringing up the topic.

Finally, on the twenty-sixth day of their engagement, Ruga took Elketh into a beautiful, peaceful forest on horseback, and they picnicked at night in the middle of a clearing to the calming sounds of hooting owls and the rustling of trees.

"This is lovely," Elketh said, closing her eyes to appreciate the feel of the breeze on her skin and the nature sounds around them. "It's not often we get out of the city."

"There's an even better forest in Sydlig," Ruga said. "Humid and hot, but it has such interesting, brightly colored birds. And monkeys. They're cute. I'll take you someday."

This was the kind of talking that made Elketh feel particularly guilty. "That sounds far. How long does it take to get there?"

"Twenty days or so from Vakker on horseback. Or we can get there quicker by taking a boat and following the coastline. There are plenty of interesting places to show you on the way, though, if we go on horseback."

A pit formed in Elketh's throat. She swallowed it with effort. Twenty days there, with stops, and twenty days back. There wasn't time for it.

She had a revelation, then, about the reason they were so busy every day when Ruga insisted she was the kind of person who liked to keep to herself. Ruga was cramming as much as she could into the time they had. A desperate attempt to show Elketh everything.

Or a persuasive attempt to make Elketh stay.

"Ruga," Elketh said, and she couldn't continue, not with those kind brown eyes on her.

"Elketh?"

"Ruga," Elketh tried again, "that trip is too long. We won't be able to go."

Ruga didn't respond right away. Elketh couldn't bear to look in her direction, to see what expression she wore.

"I know," Ruga said finally. And then, quieter, "I did say 'someday.'"

"Ruga, I'm going back to Branwen when I can." Elketh swallowed again, unbearably loud in the quiet of the clearing. She was embarrassed that her nerves could be so audible. "I'm not going to marry you."

Again, Ruga didn't respond. Seconds passed, such long seconds. Maybe this was it, then. Fear spiked in Elketh, that this would be the end of them forever. Rationally, she knew it wasn't fair to Ruga that their relationship had a time constraint and Elketh wanted it to go on until the last minute they had.

But she was advancing beyond the point of rationality.

"Ruga, did you hear me? I'm not—"

"I heard you."

"I'm really...I'm sorry. I didn't mean to pretend I was going to. I just...I needed you to know. That I haven't changed my mind."

Elketh looked over at Ruga. The orc had her hair draped over her face, expression obscured.

"I know," Ruga said.

CHAPTER TWENTY-TWO

Returning from the forest trip was awkward, and Ruga didn't know how to fix it. Part of her had pretended all along that Elketh had changed her mind already, that the tender looks they shared meant more to Elketh than she let on. It had been kind of Elketh to remind Ruga where they stood, Ruga had to remind herself.

It had been kind.

Ruga wanted time to gather her thoughts as much as she wanted to blurt out all of her overwhelming feelings. She got time to do neither. At the castle gates, the steward waited for her, tapping his foot with exaggerated impatience. "You're late," he said.

The stable boy jumped up to grab their horses. Elketh seemed all too happy to speak with him and then run away to the castle, leaving Ruga to deal with the steward alone even though they'd done everything together lately.

Ruga's eyes ached with unshed tears. "What is it?" she asked unkindly.

"You had an appointment with the queen," the steward said.

Right. Ruga had to make appointments to see her own sister. Now, she felt especially raw about that. She followed the steward into the castle, mentally preparing herself to sound pleasant, not heartbroken. First, her sister had been elected queen, forcing Ruga into a strained relationship with the closest person in her life—not to mention the eternal servitude, years and years of diplomacy.

Then, she'd had to end her romance with Hedda. It seemed so pointless now that they knew the elf king hadn't shared anything with his daughter. But the daughter had turned out to be so surprising in her own way.

Ruga's mistake was in thinking Elketh had enough time to come around, that Elketh was capable of wanting Ruga over a return to her normal life. The part that hurt the most was that Elketh had been set up to have both—both Ruga and Branwen's throne—and she only cared for one of them.

Too soon, Ruga was left alone at the doors to Astrid's ascetic rooms. At least when Ruga'd slept outside, she had an excuse to come here and catch up with Astrid as she got ready for the day. The door opened before she could knock. Astrid wrapped Ruga in a hug.

"Come in, come in."

Numbly, Ruga had a seat by Astrid's unlit fireplace in the antechamber. She accepted a too-hot cup of tea and drank it right away, barely feeling the burn on her tongue.

"Freya says things are looking up on the Elketh front," Astrid said cheerfully, pouring her own tea. How rare, for something to go well for Torden. How disappointed Astrid would be in Ruga when Astrid found out how wrong she was.

"You have faulty information," Ruga said. It was unlike Freya to lie to Astrid. Besides, the odds of Freya misinterpreting the situation were fairly low. "Elketh has asserted that she does not intend to marry me."

Astrid froze with the teacup halfway to her lips. "Hmm," she said. "I'm terribly sorry. You seem to like her. I wouldn't have guessed."

You seem to like her, Ruga thought bitterly. The words twisted like a knife. The only thing she could do was change the subject. "Where is Freya?" They called Freya "the queen's shadow" for a reason—you hardly saw Astrid without her.

"I had a surprise," Astrid said. "Although it is a bit less exciting in light of your information."

"What is it?"

"Freya will be back with it soon," Astrid said, waving Ruga off. She adjusted her crown and leaned back into her chair, sipping deeply at the tea with a sigh. "I guess we will have to use the backup plan. I hinted at it to the elvish king, and he agreed it was sensible."

Ruga stared blankly into the cold fireplace for so long that she realized too late—she was supposed to ask what the backup plan was.

"Elketh has a brother," Astrid went on anyway, setting her teacup on the tray with a tinny noise that brought Ruga back to her senses. "I've been told he's much more agreeable to his father's agendas and less difficult to deal with in general. But I wanted to ask your permission first, of course."

"My permission for what?"

"To marry the elf brother," Astrid said. "You don't have to. But...you know, I remember you telling me when we were younger that gender isn't a huge factor when it comes to love for you." Astrid paused. "Is that still true?"

"What?" Ruga asked. "Um, yes, love surpassing gender and all that."

"Great. So, what do you think?"

"Think of what?"

"Ruga, are you all right?" Astrid asked. The queen reached over to touch the back of Ruga's hand and Ruga jolted, tea sloshing over the sides of her cup onto her dress. "You seem off today."

"Is that the surprise?" Ruga asked, some semblance of clarity stabbing through her brain fog. "Our first plan fell through. Now I'm being honored with the chance to marry Elketh's brother, and Freya is coming back with him?"

Astrid was quiet, her full attention on Ruga, piercing her with those queenly eyes in a way that let Ruga know Astrid was trying to read her mind. "The surprise was more of a gesture. I'm not sure it means anything now. Especially if you don't want to marry Elketh's brother. But no. He's still in Branwen, and we only barely discussed him as an alternative when Elketh initially arrived and was reluctant. Do you need some time to think about it?"

"No," Ruga said with acid in her voice. "I'll marry whomever you want."

"Ruga, honestly! What's with you?" Astrid chastised. "You're not usually like this."

"Sorry that I can't be perfect all the time. See where it's gotten me." Miserably, Ruga blinked tears into her teacup.

Astrid's response was whisper-soft. "Stars, Ruga. You love her."

"Does it matter?"

Astrid cupped Ruga's hands in her own. "Of course it matters. I'll tell the elvish king we aren't interested."

Whether it was worth protesting—Ruga didn't feel like giving her heart away to anyone else—or continuing to serve Torden to help her sister out, Ruga couldn't say. They were interrupted by someone at the door.

“That’ll be Freya,” Astrid said. “Should I send her away?”

Freya likely knew Ruga was crying already. She would smell the salt of Ruga’s tears like a hound. “I don’t care.”

“The surprise—I thought it would be nice to give you the ceremonial crown for your wedding since all the rulers of Torden go through coronation with the thing. I believe this translates well to the Branwen alliance. You serve Torden as much as I do, if not more. You deserve to wear it during the ceremony.”

Ruga nearly choked. The initial reaction of being touched by the gesture was quickly overpowered with dread. She’d been the one to cover up the crown’s destruction, of course. It was a slap in the face to the history of her entire people.

When Freya entered the room, it was not with the ceremonial crown, although Ruga half-expected her to have dug up its hidden remains. The lady’s maid was accompanied by a very annoyed-looking Vera.

“I had to tell her,” Vera said to Ruga without greeting the queen. “You never should have asked me to keep it a secret. They were all going to find out eventually.”

“What is she talking about?” Astrid asked.

“Would you like to tell her, Ruga, or shall I?” Freya said.

Everyone looked to Ruga. She was the only one still seated, and she wished the chair would swallow her up. “The ceremonial crown is gone.”

“What does that mean, exactly?” Astrid asked.

“It means what she said. It’s been smashed up to bits,” Vera snapped. “Can I go back now?”

Panic registered on Astrid’s face. “It’s gone?”

“Yes,” Freya said, releasing Vera’s arm. Without subtlety, Vera backed toward the door. “Would you like to tell her how that happened, Ruga?”

"You're enjoying this too much," Ruga accused. She was unconvinced this was the first time Freya had heard of it—just the first time Freya had eyewitness testimony to bring to the queen. Rarely did Freya present information unless she was absolutely sure of it.

"You told Freya it was sent away to be restored," Astrid said.

"Then why did you send for it?" Ruga said, suddenly very tired.

"Vera claimed that it was back with us again."

Ruga sighed. "Really, Vera?"

"I'm a *scholar*, not your secret keeper."

"Well?" Astrid asked.

"Fine. Elketh was trying to get kicked out, and she destroyed it. I covered it up for her. Just tell people I was trying it on for the wedding and it crumbled to dust. The thing's a piece of shit anyway."

"Ruga!" Vera and Astrid said simultaneously—Vera because she was offended at the destruction of a historical artifact, and Astrid because it was crass and out of character.

A muscle worked in Astrid's jaw. "Vera, Freya. I need a word with my sister."

"Your Majesty," Vera said, almost mocking, and bowed out the door, Freya's silent footsteps following.

"I am so disappointed," Astrid said tightly. Ruga knew her sister enough to recognize that Astrid was blazing with fury. "You hid this from me."

"I didn't want it to become a big deal," Ruga said. It sounded weak even to her, like a child's excuse for bad behavior.

"I'm going to write to her father," said Astrid. "We can't have her here."

"What? No."

"It's practically an act of war." Astrid rummaged aggressively around the antechamber for paper and pen.

"That's exactly why I didn't tell you."

"And you thought I wouldn't find out?" The pen scratched the paper with an abrasive noise that set Ruga's ears on edge. Astrid crouched over a side table, writing so furiously that Ruga could see the imprint of the nib scratching through the paper and into the wood underneath.

"Not until I was gone," Ruga admitted. "Though that seems a moot point now." Like everything else.

"We will have a conversation about this later," Astrid said. "Have the couriers send this letter immediately. Even if you have to wake them up to do it."

"Yes, Your Majesty."

"And don't fucking call me that, Ruga."

Ruga took the hastily folded letter and left. It was a little bit funny, perhaps, that Astrid trusted her to deliver it. Easily, Ruga could toss the letter and pretend the encounter never happened.

Freya would know it had, though. Another letter would get to Branwen eventually.

Muscle memory carried her up the stairs rather than down to the courier. She stopped outside the door to her own rooms and pressed her palm to the wood. It was unlikely Elketh would be sitting in the antechamber, but Ruga imagined she could hear Elketh's breathing. The same breathing Ruga listened to as she fell asleep every night.

Ruga thought she should warn Elketh that the secret was out. The elvish king was so obstinate that it might not make a difference, though. Astrid could have kicked Elketh out of Torden only for Elketh to have no place back home if the king didn't want her back.

She stood there long enough that the guards in the hall cleared their throats, a nonverbal question: *Do you need help with anything?* Self-conscious of the rawness of her emotions, Ruga lowered her hand and turned away.

In the end, she didn't warn Elketh at all.

CHAPTER TWENTY-THREE

Burrowed under the covers, Elketh waited for Ruga to join her. The importance of sharing her intentions with Ruga wasn't lost on Elketh, but she hadn't decided yet if she regretted it. Ruga had taken it even worse than Elketh predicted.

And there were still all those days ahead of them before Elketh could leave.

She waited, and waited, and waited, and she practiced what she would say to Ruga. To instill what was maybe false hope: *I need more time before a lifelong commitment, but I wouldn't rule it out.* The candid option: *I don't know what the fuck I want or why I want it.*

To be completely honest with herself would be to admit that Elketh missed Ruga right that minute, and by extension, a permanent break would be nearly unbearable. But Elketh was seldom honest with herself unless she had to be.

She fretted until she fell asleep.

She woke up alone with the sun in her face.

Elketh got ready for the day with dread. Joining the castle for breakfast would be uncomfortable at best, but she had promised she wouldn't let other people know her displeasure with the betrothal. It would be suspicious for her not to show.

Someone knocked at the entrance as Elketh was giving her face a final splash from the basin. In equal turns, she wished her visitor was Ruga and hoped it wasn't. Her stomach roiled to the point where she wondered if she could handle any amount of breakfast.

Elketh slid into the antechamber, smoothing down her hair. A member of the kitchen staff waited at the door—of course, the knocking had not been Ruga's, as much as Elketh pretended she didn't know Ruga's three-rap cadence. So that was how it was going to be: Elketh was disinvited from breakfast.

She was so distraught at this that she registered too late that this was not someone from the kitchen staff but a smallish orc boy wearing the blue wool of the courier service.

"A letter for you," he said, and held it out to her.

Elketh turned the thin paper over in her hands. She recognized the formal handwriting on the envelope. "From whom?" she asked, because she had to hear it said.

"King Gareth."

Her father's seal stared up at her from the back of the letter. There were faint imprints along each of the four sides, like it had been tied with twine to another note or perhaps a package of some sort. With a fingernail, she broke the seal. The paper trembled in her hands as she held it up.

Daughter,

I thought that your time with the orcs would improve your character. It is to my great disappointment that you are just as much of an embarrassment as you ever were. I am sending the ferry to fetch you in the afternoon. Have your things packed and be ready at the harbor. You have caused all of Branwen much disgrace. I am ashamed to call you my kin.

What circumstances led you to the destruction of a sacred object, I cannot even begin to comprehend. As a representative of our country, your lack of respect for Torden is a lack of respect for Branwen, and as such, you are no longer my heir. From now on, you will best serve Branwen as support for your brother's future rule. I hope the consequences of your actions will cause some reflection and remorse on your part.

The letter was not signed, and Elketh's father loved signing letters with his big signature. That's how Elketh really knew she was in trouble.

So they'd found out about the crown she smashed to bits. It was a miracle that it had taken this long, but somehow, Elketh had felt some false sense of security as time passed, as though having not been caught yet meant she would never be.

She glanced up and found the courier was long gone. Breakfast could wait. Not entirely processing the letter yet, Elketh stepped to the wardrobe and extracted the dresses she liked the most, setting them on the back of Ruga's writing chair in a pile. She would have to get a trunk somewhere to transport them.

I'm going home, she realized. This was what she'd wanted all along. She made no attempt to constrain the excitement that flooded her at the thought of returning to Branwen with its beautiful green hills and beautiful elf women. Her old life had been good.

The life she had here wasn't bad. She had gotten used to it, had liked certain aspects of it. This was better, though. The choice was being made for her. She didn't have to be the one to break Ruga's heart over her indecisiveness, and Ruga would be free of her obligations to Elketh. Elketh knew well how much of a handful she could be.

Maybe Ruga would go back to Hedda, Elketh thought, and the mental image of the two of them together left her queasy.

But this way was kinder to Ruga. Ruga had always deserved better than Elketh, Elketh had to admit, and Elketh's own whims ran too wild for Ruga's stable nature. If Elketh's history was any indication, the return home would quickly absolve her of any remorse over what could have been. And while Elketh's father claimed he was no longer giving her his throne, she was sure it was a passing phase. He could overcome it. The letter had been two entire paragraphs, after all, and he only sent bad news without minced words. She would just have to be on good behavior for a bit, and then he would suggest marrying her off to someone else, and she could rule like she'd wanted to since she was a girl.

And Ruga could stay here in the homeland that she loved so much.

Optimistic that she could change her father's mind, Elketh packed with renewed fervor, her hands trembling uncontrollably.

CHAPTER TWENTY-FOUR

Ruga pushed around the food on her plate with no intention of eating it. There was an empty spot on the bench next to her. She felt that the open space was a kindred spirit with herself: empty, empty, empty, and purposeless, too.

The only thing Ruga had space for in her stomach this morning was worries. She worried that things would never be the same with Elketh; she worried that Elketh would be exiled from Torden without anywhere to go; she worried that every meaningful connection she'd ever had was dissipating like fog.

"From Branwen," someone was saying. "How interesting is that?"

"Whyever would they send a ferry today?" the guard next to the steward asked. "Should we be worried about something nefarious?"

"No," Astrid said. "We received a letter from the elvish king today. He is retrieving his daughter." The queen spared Ruga a troubled glance.

Ruga's heart sank into her stomach.

"Is he reneging on the alliance?" the steward asked, appalled. The bench beneath Ruga groaned as everyone bent toward the conversation, even as they pretended not to pay attention.

"It's voluntary," said the queen. "We've come up with another arrangement. We will still have Branwen's support if Lynby chooses to move against us."

"That's a relief," the guard said. "It does beg the question of why they bothered trying to marry our Ruga off in the first place." At *our Ruga*, Ruga felt the gazes of several people on her at once.

"Indeed. We were already breaking convention for them," said the steward.

Of course the steward would need to know about an incoming ferry, but it felt like betrayal that Ruga had to find out in public. She'd spent another uncomfortable night in the rose garden, another morning getting ready in her sister's rooms, this time in silence. If Astrid knew, she could have told Ruga, but she'd chosen not to.

Ruga excused herself from the table. The ferry was coming *today*. She knew she would regret if she didn't see Elketh one last time.

Three steps at a time, Ruga dashed up the stairs. Out of breath, Ruga entered her bedchamber to the sight of Elketh humming as she gleefully stacked up the dresses Ruga had commissioned.

"Oh!" Elketh said when she saw Ruga. She stepped back from the dresses, fabric on fabric layered like an elaborate cake. "Ruga."

"Good morning," Ruga said, the first thing to pop into her head.

"My father's sent a ferry to be here by the afternoon," Elketh said. She resumed stacking up dresses. Ruga eyed one of her own traveling trunks stuffed with them. "I'm in trouble for breaking the ceremonial crown."

"I know," Ruga said. "You...just started packing?"

"I've been packing for some time," Elketh said, stretching up into the wardrobe on the tips of her toes to reach the neckband Ruga had bought her. There was a frenetic energy about her that clashed with Ruga's own mood.

"Are you going to fight it?" Ruga forced herself to say.

"What do you mean?" Elketh asked. She shoved the trunk closed. It bounced back up at her, overfull of fabrics—all of which the townspeople of Torden had made by hand.

"You're just going to leave and not come back?"

Elketh stopped shoving at the trunk. There was a reddish tuft from one of the dresses sticking out of her hair; Ruga reached out and plucked it away. Elketh stared at the tuft and licked her lips. "Ruga... I told you that I've wanted to go back the entire time I've been here."

Suddenly, Ruga felt very dizzy. She sat on the edge of the bed. "I can come with you. That was—that was the original plan, anyway."

"I'm not the heir anymore," Elketh said, in a way that indicated she didn't really believe it. "There's no reason to take you away from Torden."

How to explain to Elketh that Ruga wanted change? That she felt stuck here? That leaving to help another country clearly in need of a power shift was something that would give Ruga purpose?

That Elketh made it worth staying in a diplomatic role for the rest of Ruga's life?

"You can tell him that you consent to the betrothal," Ruga tried, her voice cracking. "If you decide you don't want me later, I'll leave." Even to Ruga's ears, it sounded desperate. Pleading.

"Oh, Ruga, I couldn't do that to you," Elketh said. She didn't move from her trunk on the floor, didn't look up at Ruga's teary eyes. "I don't want to hurt you, but I have to speak plainly."

A minute of awkward silence ensued, during which all of Ruga's muscles tensed. "Are you asking my permission to speak plainly?"

Elketh's eyes hardened. "I guess not. I don't want to marry you, Ruga, and I never did. We can stay in touch, though. Visit each other. I would like that."

They hadn't known each other long, but Ruga understood Elketh well enough to recognize the lie. "You would go back to your normal life," Ruga said, her voice rising, "and forget about me. You wouldn't come visit me. I would cross the channel for you, and it would be a one-way trip just to be one of your many conquests."

Elketh's mouth fell open. "Ruga, that's not fair."

What wasn't fair was Ruga making sacrifices over and over again for people who didn't appreciate them. Her lips pursed. She held the thoughts in. Elketh had made up her mind, and it wasn't going to change. Ruga could cry later, but not in front of Elketh.

From the floor, Elketh let out an exaggerated sigh. "It's been lovely here, Ruga. This could have been much worse. And no matter what kind of relationship you want to have with me, I'll always remember you."

Every sentence cut deeply. Ruga turned her head away and tried to think of anything: the midsummer festivals, the waves lapping at the shore, the blacksmith's forge. Everything reminded her of Elketh. Just yesterday morning they'd been fine, or so it had seemed. Only when Ruga started pushing had Elketh pulled back.

It also seemed like the only thing keeping Elketh close to Ruga was a stubborn elvish king. Their entire relationship unfurled before Ruga, souring in her mind and her heart. "I have to go," she said abruptly. She rushed to the door.

"Wait, Ruga?"

Ruga froze as Elketh's hand curled over Ruga's shoulder. Clenching her fists, Ruga resisted the urge to reach up and hold it.

"I want you to be there with me at the harbor. So we can say goodbye," Elketh said.

A forever goodbye. Ruga felt pathetic. Even now, she wouldn't deny Elketh anything.

Maybe this whole thing was her fault. By not speaking up earlier—not speaking up about what she wanted, not speaking up to warn Elketh about her impending departure—she'd ruined everything. Who else was there to blame? Elketh hadn't been vague about her intentions.

Ruga's fickle heart was the only thing that had caused all this hurt.

"All right," Ruga said, but she still shrugged out from under Elketh's grip and left.

She would have that little power of her own, at least.

CHAPTER TWENTY-FIVE

Elketh was back home, and it was everything she had imagined.

First, she took extra time to laze around outside, breathing in the fresh air of the rolling green hills where she'd grown up. The archery station near Ceridwen Hold wasn't as good as the one in Torden; she went hunting instead and brought home a fat rabbit. Surprisingly, her father had no orders for her, no obligations. She'd only seen him once, when she arrived at Branwen's shore, and he had nodded at her presence from a distance to acknowledge her return. There had been no fanfare.

She carried the rabbit in one fist and tried not to think about the forlorn look on Ruga's face as the orc watched Elketh board the ferry. When it was time to part, Elketh had held her arms open to Ruga for one last embrace—and she was convinced the only reason Ruga reciprocated was because others were present, and Ruga didn't want Elketh to be embarrassed. It was a stiff, uncomfortable hug, the hug of strangers. Not of two people who had spent the last few weeks physically and emotionally intertwined.

Still, Ruga had stayed on the shore, watching, long after everyone else in the queen's retinue had left.

Elketh thought to stop by her old lovers' dwellings, but she didn't feel right doing it just yet. She'd had plenty of sex recently, in any case, and didn't need it right now, but as soon as she was readjusted, she was sure she'd jump back into her old habits.

The rabbit bounced limply in her grip, its ears flopping. It was a beautiful day.

After she was sated with flexing her archery skills and running through the hills, Elketh returned to the castle, her muscles burning. The dining hall was dark. She'd forgotten that Ceridwen Hold didn't host a grand dinner every night unless there were important guests. It would have been nice if they'd set up a celebration for her return, though.

She greeted several of the servants as she passed them. To her dismay, each one startled at her presence. "Princess Elketh," one of them said, bowing. Everyone else was very busy, rushing away to fulfill some urgent chore as soon as Elketh greeted them. Very well, Elketh thought. It had been a while since she ate something she'd made herself. She headed back outside and started a fire over which to cook the rabbit and began to dress it.

The conversation with Ruga could have gone differently, Elketh supposed as she turned the spit to roast her rabbit. If Elketh had suggested keeping up their relationship from their respective countries first, it might not have gone over so poorly. The trip across the channel was short. Ruga's implication that Elketh should fight the forced return was a shock to Elketh, to whom it had not occurred to resist.

Maybe it would have been easier on both of them if Elketh had let their relationship end naturally—if they visited each other once a month, then once every two, then three, until they were able to overcome whatever inconvenient feelings had developed between them. Elketh knew well how quitting a dalliance cold turkey could lead to angry lovers pounding on the castle doors until the steward shooed them away with a broom.

Why hadn't Elketh thought it through? She was more calculated than this when it came to her love life. And her first instinct was always to defy her father. Something about Ruga had thrown her off, and she didn't like it.

In any case, enough time alone would help Ruga realize she was better off without Elketh dragging her down. But they could have worked something out, perhaps.

If Elketh wanted their relationship to work out, which she wasn't sure she did.

The rabbit was a tad overcooked when Elketh eased it off the spit. She'd been somewhat lost in thought for most of the cooking process and had not noticed it burning. Her next rabbit would be better, and she could plan ahead to share it with one of her many friends.

By the time Elketh finished eating the rabbit, she was annoyed that no one had come to find her. She could admit to herself that she liked being the center of attention, though she didn't by any means *need* to be. What she hated was not getting any attention at all, and it felt like she was being actively ignored.

There had to be someone who wanted to talk to her.

An hour later, after cleaning herself off, Elketh arrived at her brother's rooms. If he was busy, she planned to unload the trunks with all the dresses and spend a great deal of time organizing them by color.

She should have asked Ruga if it was okay to take them, she realized as she knocked.

"Come in!" Owain called. Elketh entered the room. See, she thought. Everything would go back to normal.

"How have you been, Owain? I missed you."

Owain grunted. He was splayed out in a chair, reading a book. "Did you really?"

"Of course," Elketh said. She was sure she'd thought of him at least once or twice. "What are you reading?"

"Reading up on Torden's history," he said. "It's pretty interesting. If you liked to read, I might lend it to you next."

"I like to read fine," Elketh said sourly as she took a seat in the matching chair. "I read in Torden sometimes. Why are you reading about an orc country?"

Owain glanced up from the book and back down. He'd had a haircut since the last time she saw him, and his pointed ears poked straight out more than usual, like they did when he was irritated. "You know that I'm going to be the king of Branwen now, don't you?"

"Yes," Elketh said.

"I wasn't sure how much Father told you. He said he was angry and embarrassed and didn't wish to speak with you."

"He told me everything." Or so she'd like to think; that Owain would be privy to knowledge Elketh didn't have upset her too much to consider.

"Great," Owain said. "You owe me for this, Elketh. I never meant to rule, and I have a lot of catching up to do."

Catching up to things Elketh never bothered learning in the first place. Owain had centered his learning around his interests; they expected that he'd marry off and move away at some point. Elketh supposed that was in store for her in the near future. It was a little ironic, wasn't it, that she'd gotten what she wanted by returning to Branwen early, but she would have to live somewhere else as soon as her new partner was picked out?

"Is there any chance he would change his mind?" Elketh asked.

"Doubtful. He's pissed," Owain said. "What did you think of Princess Ruga?"

"She's fine. Normal," Elketh said, shoving thoughts of Ruga as far away from her as she could. She did not come up here to talk about Ruga. "How is Rhiannon?"

"Her betrothal to Fiona was announced while you were gone," he said. "Fiona's already in Olwen."

"Rhiannon is getting married? That's a damn shame. Although, I don't know a Fiona," Elketh admitted.

"You do know her," said Owain. "You just can't ever remember her name."

Elketh racked her brain. "*Fipple?* She gets to marry Rhiannon?" The world was an unfair place, indeed.

"What about Princess Ruga?" Owain asked again.

"Why do you need to know about her?" Elketh asked. The answer was already dawning on her, though—why else would Owain need to read about Torden?

"As soon as the embarrassment about you has died down," Owain said, "I'm going to marry her instead. Probably a year from now or so, Father said. That's plenty of time for me to do some research."

Blood rushed in Elketh's ears. Owain, given a year to prepare; Elketh, given fifteen minutes. Owain, marrying Ruga; Elketh, not marrying Ruga, but having to see Ruga and Owain together in Ceridwen Hold for the rest of her life.

"Wow, is she that bad?" Owain asked.

Elketh blinked rapidly. "Sorry?"

"You look like someone slapped you."

"I—no, she's not bad at all. She's good. Kind." Elketh fiddled with a lock of her hair. Had Ruga touched the same strands today, mere hours ago?

Ruga was *wrong*. Elketh would have visited her in Torden.

"That's a relief," Owain said. "I didn't think I'd be marrying an orc, but I'm glad she's kind."

"Did—ah—does she know yet?" Elketh asked. She had the impression that she was floating outside of her body, watching the conversation from above.

"Yes," Owain said. "She's agreed to it already."

"Ah," Elketh said. "Um. I should get going. I smell like rabbit."

Owain set his book down, marking his place with a thumb. "You smell like rabbit? What are you on about?" And then: "Elketh, why are you crying?"

Elketh wiped at her eyes. She was fine. Time healed everything, and she had plenty of time. If Ruga wanted to marry Owain, that was her choice. Elketh's father had promised them an alliance, and Torden needed the extra military power if they ever went to war with Lynby. It was perfectly rational.

"I cooked the rabbit myself. It was smoky, that's all."

Owain looked skeptical. As Elketh's chin began to wobble, she excused herself and headed to her own rooms. The dresses wouldn't unpack themselves.

She would get over Ruga with time. She had to.

CHAPTER TWENTY-SIX

Vakker Castle had never been so busy. Any opportunity for Ruga to process her feelings slipped through her fingers before she even realized it was there. Ruga ran errands for the queen which seemed to eat up entire days, and the rest of the time, she was being looped into side projects, helping out the seamstress Dag finish up an order of dresses and assisting the blacksmith in crafting a complicated armor set for a new recruit of the queen's félag.

"I'm glad you're not leaving until next year," the blacksmith said on Ruga's third long evening in the scorching hot forge. "It's been great to have an extra set of hands. We may need you if the time comes."

If the time comes, the blacksmith said, because most of Torden's citizens were scared to mention war explicitly out of superstition that mentioning it would bring Lynby's strongest warriors over the wall that separated their countries. In any case, if Lynby's warlords attacked Torden, Ruga would be present, helping her sister lead armies. It was promised, now, that Ruga would marry Owain of Branwen instead, and she was only a little relieved when Freya informed her that the brother was already aware and willing to marry her.

The thing about keeping busy was that Ruga had just enough brainpower to be sad and not enough to really think through why she was sad or what she could do about it. She bit back sudden tears in the presence of others, and sleep was no escape—not in the bedchamber Elketh had slept in. Ruga changed the sheets out, but she swore she could still smell Elketh's hair oil whenever a light breeze swept through the room. There was an indelible stain on the wall where Elketh had splashed ink in some fit of rage. Ruga ran her fingers over the stain and found evenly spaced notches underneath where Elketh had tallied the passage of time. There were seventeen marks in sets of five with two stragglers.

What had happened that seventeenth day? She tortured herself with wondering. Was that when they'd first had sex, or was it when they'd gone to the festival? Or maybe it was earlier—when Elketh destroyed the ceremonial crown, and she'd been sure she would get sent home right away, and so there was no need to count?

Did Elketh ceasing to count the days mean she didn't feel trapped in Torden anymore? Or had she really hated it the whole time?

People danced around mentioning Elketh, at least to Ruga's face (she was sure there were plenty of theories for Elketh's departure behind her back). Every time Ruga tried to engage at dinner, it seemed like there was a great gap, conversations that shaped themselves around an absence. A question on everyone's minds: *Did something else really happen?* They'd been publicly chummy with one another, and anyone who witnessed Hedda's great outburst knew that they'd been intimate, too.

Hedda was another thing Ruga didn't know what to do about. With Elketh gone, it was especially apparent how much Ruga missed Hedda's presence in her life. Rekindling their relationship seemed like a bad idea—there was an expiration date on it, after all, whenever Ruga and Owain married.

Guiltily, Ruga considered whether Hedda would be open to a more casual type of fling. It wasn't lost on her that those were the kinds of relationships Elketh preferred.

The guardroom on the queen's floor was quiet when Ruga came to visit a week and some days after Elketh's departure. As captain of the félag, Hedda stayed close to the queen's suite in case of disaster or emergency. There were guards stationed on every floor.

It was nighttime. Inconvenient for people who needed to be on their toes early in the morning. She considered turning around, but someone had already noticed her from the candle-lit tables next to the bunked beds, where two guards played a game of Tafl. The guards slept in shifts to provide full coverage of Vakker Castle. Those awake were in their gambesons, ready to don armor if needed.

"Do you need something?" they asked. Their companion looked up at Ruga and gave her a little wave. Visits to Hedda had been frequent in the past, and as a result, Ruga knew many of the guards well.

"I wanted to talk to Hedda," Ruga said before she could lose her nerve. "Is she sleeping?"

"She's not," came Hedda's voice from one of the bunks. Ruga stood still as Hedda entered the circle of light from the candle. As though awaiting a military command, Hedda opened her stance and held her hands in front of her. Her chin-length hair was a bit mussed. Ruga had woken up many mornings to that same hair on the pillow beside her. It was faintly blue, almost greenish in the room's lighting.

"This isn't a formal visit," Ruga clarified.

Hedda tilted her head. "Would you like to go for a walk?"

It was a disgustingly muggy night as Ruga and Hedda followed the path along the outside of the castle, carefully avoiding the rose garden. Walks were familiar to Ruga and Hedda over the course of their romance. The act was strange now, like retracing steps on a road that no longer existed. Their steps, as they always had been, were perpetually out of sync, Ruga's casual saunter contrasting with Hedda's crisp military stride. In a way, this was the only communication between them; since Hedda suggested the walk, the two hadn't exchanged a word.

Ruga was fabricating an excuse to head back inside when Hedda broke the silence. "I never had the chance to say that I'm sorry for how I behaved at the solstice."

"Oh," Ruga said. She hadn't come for an apology.

"I behaved stupid and childish. I shouldn't have approached you, and I shouldn't have had that much to drink, either. I embarrassed myself and both you and the elf princess."

"She's gone now," Ruga said. "It hardly matters."

Obligingly, Hedda smiled. "That's kind of you to say, Ruga. But it does matter to me, and it matters to the queen."

Right—Hedda was still scrubbing floors before she could have breakfast. "I'll have her take you off of cleaning duty. It wasn't completely your fault."

Distracted, Hedda bobbed her head. Her messy hair fell into her eyes.

"Do you resent her?" Ruga asked gently.

"Queen Astrid? Yes." A blunt, quick answer. "You and I would still be together if she hadn't accepted the marriage alliance."

We could be together again, Ruga thought to say. She imagined kissing Hedda—Hedda pushing her up against the stone wall like when they used to sneak away while the castle was sleeping. But Ruga could only picture herself with Elketh instead, Elketh's hands and Elketh's moans and Elketh's feather-soft elvish ears.

Actually, Ruga hadn't lied to Elketh: she didn't harbor feelings for Hedda anymore.

"I resent you, too," Hedda said. "A little." At least she was honest.

Ruga nodded, accepting this. "You swore fealty to Astrid," Ruga said. "She trusted you more than anyone."

"Not more than *anyone*," Hedda said. She didn't mean Ruga.

Ruga tried a different angle. "We need the extra support."

"Everyone is always saying that," Hedda said, waving her hand in dismissal. "We have a much more organized military force here than those slipshod warlords." Hedda stopped walking so abruptly that Ruga almost slammed into her. "You didn't come to me to talk politics."

"I didn't," Ruga admitted.

"Then what?"

The reasons were purely selfish, Ruga realized. Hedda didn't deserve to be burdened with them.

"You miss Elketh," Hedda said. It was the first time Hedda had said Elketh's name in front of Ruga.

"Yes."

"And you thought being around me would help."

Ruga sighed. "Yes."

"Is it working?"

"I don't know yet," Ruga said. And then, before she could lose her nerve: "I really miss you."

"I miss you too," Hedda said, snorting. "Otherwise, I wouldn't have made such an ass of myself."

"Where does that leave us?" Ruga asked, and then stepped back, shocked, an invasive memory of asking Elketh the same question overwhelming her.

"I would like to forgive you," Hedda said. She twisted the thick ring of the queen's félag around her finger. "I don't know how long it will take." Hedda looked up at Ruga with so much emotion in her eyes that it left Ruga breathless.

This was what had attracted Ruga to Hedda in the first place. Ruga was drawn to people who burned with so much passion that you could hardly look at them, those strong enough to go to any ends to get what they wanted.

This was also what drew Ruga to Elketh.

She had a moment of clarity, standing there in silence with Hedda. Elketh, jumping into the harbor to get back home. Elketh, destroying property to be exiled. Elketh, waking Ruga to take a chance on something romantic between them.

Sometimes, Ruga felt so steady that she could scream. She needed a fiery person to balance her out.

She supposed, also, this was the thing that had been most painful about Elketh leaving. If Elketh had really wanted Ruga, she would have gone to an extreme length to have her, but she'd surrendered to her father's wishes instead. This was why Ruga was so sure Elketh wanted to be back home more than she wanted her. Why she was so sure that, between the two of them, Ruga was the only one moping.

Chest physically hurting, Ruga coughed to cover her feelings. Her throat was clogged with emotion. “I’m sorry, Hedda,” she said, and Hedda understood her, as Hedda often did.

“I hope there’s a way you two can be together,” Hedda said with effort, still twisting her ring. “I’m going back to sleep now.”

“Thank you, Hedda,” Ruga said as Hedda walked away.

Hedda turned back and gave Ruga a mournful little smile. “You’re welcome.”

CHAPTER TWENTY-SEVEN

"How does that look, my lady?" Isolde asked.

Elketh turned her head in the mirror, admiring her freshly braided coiffure. The plaits draped down either side of her face, framing her protruding elvish ears and intertwining prettily in the back. Pins studded with amber held everything in place. "It looks great, Isolde. Thank you."

Isolde fluffed up the ends of Elketh's hair. "I like that neckband. Did you get it in Torden?"

Inhaling sharply, Elketh traced the intricate branches of the neckband with her fingers. Now that she was home, falling into her old routines, it was almost like she'd never been to Torden at all. She needed these tangible reminders. "Yes."

"The craftsmanship is excellent."

Elketh held her breath as Isolde dabbed grease from her nose. The maid stepped back, lifting Elketh's chin with one finger to check her handiwork.

"Beautiful as ever," Isolde said. "Are you ready to go to dinner?"

They were hosting a banquet tonight in the dining hall, the first since Elketh's homecoming. She wasn't sure how she felt about it yet—the king made it clear that the feast was in honor of a visiting earl and his retinue. More than likely an intentional slight against her. "I suppose."

Isolde bit her lip, considering voicing something Elketh wouldn't like, if Elketh knew her at all after the many years of her service. "If you don't mind me saying, you seem different."

Elketh's expression shuttered. "How so?"

As though bracing for Elketh's wrath, Isolde hopped a dainty step back. "I was going to say kinder," Isolde said. "But less boisterous than you were. What did they do to you over there?"

They had done nothing. Or perhaps it was Elketh who had done nothing. Elketh dismissed Isolde so the maid had a chance to eat, too, and spent several minutes staring at the reflection of her neck.

The dining hall in Ceridwen Hold, Elketh had never noticed before, was lifeless, even full of people.

As she took her seat next to her brother, she thought what a shame it was that everyone sat next to each other in separate chairs, isolated, instead of thigh-to-thigh, shaking an entire bench with every laugh. And how odd it was that the skald here recited the same poems over and over without musical accompaniment. And how dull to be served a plate of food with predetermined portions, a cup filled at regular half-hour intervals with watered-down wine. The ceilings stretched too high up, and the stark white walls were decorated with the lifeless art of rulers past, as was common for elf nobility.

Everywhere, Elketh perceived that her father's traditions were antithetical to the way things should be.

All down the table, everyone behaved as though nothing had changed. For the first time ever, Elketh felt out of place here, like she didn't belong, and she started to question if she ever had. Her eyes darted around the room, taking in sights she was accustomed to her whole life and only thinking how they could be improved, how much better they were somewhere else. Her brother made a crass joke that garnered him giggles from his friends and a stern look from their father—had he always been so immature? He was the role model child, and she was the unruly one. That was how it had always been.

The day after their conversation, Owain had checked on Elketh to dig at the source of her poorly hidden melancholy, but she hadn't been in the mood for sharing—she didn't know, precisely, what there *was* to share.

But she was getting dreadfully, awfully close.

"Excuse me. I have a headache," Elketh announced to the table. She garnered from several expressions as she stood to leave that no one quite believed her.

Isolde was already in Elketh's rooms when Elketh arrived. The maid startled at Elketh's presence.

"Are you unwell?" asked Isolde.

"Quite," said Elketh. She sat at her vanity, rubbing makeup from her face with a rag. "What in the world is this?"

A bouquet of flowers arranged on a golden tray graced her vanity, with a little card tented next to them. Bleary-eyed, Elketh picked up the card and read: *For your consideration. Love, Wanda of Anwen.*

"From a suitor," Isolde said unnecessarily. "You are an eligible bachelorette again."

Wanda. It took Elketh a moment to place her. She was a pretty elf, although a little timid, from the few times Elketh had met her. Anwen was a smaller island than Branwen or Olwen, and considerably less powerful. That her father would entertain a courtship between Elketh and Wanda was an insult more than anything else. Elketh could do worse, though, as far as she was concerned. It was a rational choice to make.

Then again, Elketh was not known for her rational choices.

Elketh went to pick up the flowers and hissed as she pricked her finger on a thorn. A bead of crimson welled up on the pad of her thumb. Numbly, she gawked at it, even as Isolde rushed forward to wipe the blood away.

"Why wouldn't they cut the thorns off of the roses first?" Isolde complained.

Roses.

Roses.

"Isolde," Elketh rasped, "I'm afraid I've made a terrible mistake."

"Whatever do you mean?" Isolde asked. "Princess Elketh? Elketh!"

"Help me break into my father's study," Elketh said. She was now holding a very sharp, very thin hunting knife.

"That doesn't sound like a good idea."

But Elketh was already halfway down the hall, breezing past servants to her father's study. When Elketh slid the knife into the padlock on the door, wiggling it around, she heard Isolde's reluctant footsteps join her.

"Have you done this often?" Isolde asked in a hoarse whisper.

The door creaked open. Elketh swept into the room, her thoughts a jumble. "Do you know where he would keep letters?"

"Letters, my lady?"

"Letters! You've worked for him forever. Help me. Please."

It wasn't long before Elketh ransacked the entire study. Elketh slammed open drawers, ripped books from the shelves, and rifled through papers—boring, boring papers in which people made their best attempts at currying the king's favor. For her part, Isolde searched just enough to be considered technically "helpful" without engaging in any of Elketh's destruction.

"Princess Elketh," Isolde said after Elketh had ripped open a couch cushion with her knife, "your father keeps a locked drawer at his desk."

Elketh sprung for it. The lock was too intricate for her knife to handle. She stabbed the sharp end of the knife into the top, severing the locking mechanism from the inside with jagged cuts of the oak.

When she saw the damage, Isolde looked as though she would faint. "Oh, Princess, what have you done?"

From the drawer, Elketh lifted a thick stack of letters bundled with twine. They were the ones she'd sent to Branwen, beseeching distant family and lovers for help. It irritated her that her father had them all delivered directly to him. No wonder nobody had responded. She tossed the stack aside, flipping through records of the earls' estates until she'd just about given up.

"I can't find it," Elketh said aloud. "Oh, stars, Isolde, I can't find it."

"Princess," Isolde said gently, "what are you looking for?"

And then Elketh saw it: a corner of folded paper wedged into the back of the drawer. As gingerly as she had the patience for, Elketh tugged it loose. The paper fell open in her shaking hands, and her eyes roved over it, starting at the middle and jumping back up to the top, so frantic she could hardly process the words.

Princess Elketh of Branwen—

Greetings! My name is Ruga Karrsdaughter, though I go by Ruga. I'm pleased that we're engaged to be married.

My sister recommended that I tell you a little about myself, which I thought was a splendid idea. I was born into a merchant family, and I'm relatively well-traveled. I've never been to Branwen, but I have visited Olwen's trading hubs, and the landscape was quite beautiful. During the nomadic lifestyle of my youth, I encountered many craftspeople, the most talented blacksmiths and weavers and carpenters you'll ever meet, and I picked up a few things from them, so I have a wide variety of skills to bring with me to Branwen. I'm also very fond of gardening.

The fifty-day engagement is a new concept to me, but I'm so very glad to have the chance to show you around Torden before I join you for good on your island. It's a place I'm proud to call my home. You'll be here for our midsummer celebration, too—one of my favorite times of the year. I can't wait to experience it together.

It's so hard to represent yourself in a letter. To be honest, I've written many drafts of this one. Arranged marriage is foreign to me, so I'm a bit apprehensive. The good thing, naturally, is that an arranged marriage necessitates learning the ropes with someone else.

I'm ready to experience new things at your side.

Soon-to-be yours,

—Ruga

Elketh gasped for air. She read it once and then again to make sure she hadn't missed anything. She thought she would choke. If Ruga had been earnest—and Elketh had been sure Ruga *was*—that meant that Ruga had sincerely been ready to disrupt her life, uproot it, and change it forever, and Elketh had not.

"Princess, what's the matter?" Isolde asked, reaching for Elketh's arm.

Elketh clutched the letter to her aching chest and forced herself to acknowledge her emotions. Regret. What she was feeling was regret. "I shouldn't have left."

"Why did you?" Isolde asked, swallowing. Elketh knew the maids gossiped about the new arrangement with Owain and Elketh's sudden return, and they'd been nearly right, guessing that

Elketh disgraced herself but not how. After all, Elketh had a reputation around Ceridwen Hold.

The destruction of the ceremonial crown was something Elketh genuinely regretted, but the demand for her return after her father found out was a perfect excuse to return to the life she knew.

"Because I'm scared of change," Elketh whispered, and then clapped her hands over her mouth at the depth of her honesty. It set in, then, what needed to be done. "Isolde, I'm about to do something very brash, and I recommend you leave now so you can pretend you were never involved."

Aghast, Isolde gestured to the mess of the study. "Can it be any worse than this?"

Elketh rushed past Isolde into the hallway, down the winding stairs, so quickly she upended a servant carrying a tray of food. She nearly slipped in the spilled stew but trudged on, out the castle, past two startled guards, darting between people at the docks, her lungs working so hard she felt they could burst, until she was at the harbor, taking great, heaving breaths.

"Princess!" Isolde screamed from somewhere behind her. "What do you think you're doing?"

Elketh slashed at the ropes mooring a fishing boat to the harbor. She pushed it out into the water and hopped in.

"Elketh!" Isolde cried out over the body of water, her voice echoing all around them.

Settling each oar into place, Elketh began to row.

CHAPTER TWENTY-EIGHT

The head of a white rose tumbled into Ruga's hand.

It wasn't the smartest thing to do, pruning roses at night, but she had brought an extra lantern, and she was too busy to do it during the day, and she had spent less time in the garden than usual. Ruga located the next rose that needed to be snipped, collecting the heads in a shallow basket. She thought she would use them to have a luxurious rose-petal bath before she went to bed.

For a moment, she forgot all her troubles, and then she heard a distinctive string of squeaks. Ruga squinted into the sky, into the broad wingspan of a peregrine falcon.

"Freya?" she called.

There was the sound of a knife crunching into something wet. Ruga turned. Hidden in the corner of the garden, the queen's shadow—without her queen—splayed out on an eiderdown blanket as though for a picnic. She had an apple in one hand and her carved bone-handled dagger in the other.

"Want a slice?" offered Freya.

"How long have you been there?"

Freya lifted her gauntleted arm, still holding the apple, for the falcon to land. She stroked the falcon's feathery head with a gloved forefinger, the knife between her thumb and her palm. "Not long," she said. "Just wanted to chat. I have a confession to make."

Ruga pushed down the unease that crawled up her throat. "And what would that be?"

The dagger sliced into the apple again. Freya lifted a neat, thin wedge and slipped it between her lips. "I convinced King Gareth to reach out about the betrothal to the elvish princess."

Sometimes, it seemed like Freya had control over everything. It shouldn't have surprised Ruga, and yet... "Did you really? Why?"

Freya nodded, attempting to feed a piece of apple to the falcon, who was very much uninterested. "If Torden gets into the hands of the Lynby warlords, they'll come for Branwen next. They're interested in expansion. Branwen's an influential island but easy to secure with the right strategy. I let him know the consequences of such a takeover. Told him what I thought they would try. He's personally invested."

That was Freya for you. She didn't lie, exactly, but she played on your worst fears. Did it change anything, that the engagement was orchestrated?

"To be frank, I thought the king would want to marry his daughter to someone else, but from what he told me of the elf princess, she did seem like your type," said Freya. "Although, I did not anticipate the king going to such extremes to get her here. He underplayed how difficult she would be. He was so sure she would come around."

Ruga clenched and unclenched her fist. The elvish king clearly did not understand his daughter as well as he thought he had. "And my sister? Did she know you orchestrated this?"

"I encouraged her to agree to it, of course."

"You manipulated her," Ruga accused.

At this, Freya flung the dagger into the ground, where it stuck, wobbling. The falcon took flight at her anger. "I was completely transparent with the queen, as I *always* am. She gave me her blessing to speak with the elvish king. I have her best interests in mind. She would tell you the same."

That, Ruga did believe. "I guess not all of your plans work out."

Freya's brow furrowed. She turned the apple—missing a quarter of its mass—over in her gloved hands. "No. Not all of them."

"I suppose you think telling me this is going to make me feel better?" Ruga asked.

"I thought it might help with something," said Freya.

"It's not."

"It will."

Sighing, Ruga gathered up her basket with its roses. "I'm heading back in."

"I wouldn't if I were you."

"Why not?"

"There's a boat coming for you." It was a saying that referred to the boat ride to the goddess's field, where people went after death before they were reincarnated. Freya cupped a hand over her eyes as though trying to see a far distance away.

"Stop being cryptic," Ruga said, losing patience. Whatever peace she'd gained from being in the rose garden was long gone.

"It's a literal boat." Sharply, Freya grinned, and Ruga could tell that Freya took some pleasure in the wordplay. "So you stay here. Keep working on those roses."

"A boat?" Ruga asked. "Did the seer tell you that?"

"Maybe," Freya said. She rose from the blanket. From wherever she'd been watching, the falcon returned to Freya's gauntlet.

"Are you going to take your nice blanket with you?" Ruga asked, petulant, as Freya turned to go.

"Brenn said you'd need that, too."

"It's awfully warm for eiderdown."

Freya didn't have a response for that. She was already gone.

Ruga began to fold up the blanket. Part of Freya's demeanor was deliberate intimidation, a power struggle that always left Ruga feeling confused at best and diminished at worst. It was designed to make the other party succumb to Freya's will, and thus, the queen's. Technically, it was harmless, so long as you hadn't made an enemy of Astrid. But that didn't make Ruga feel better.

As far as Ruga knew, the seer Brenn had never had a vision about her. Hopefully, Freya didn't plan for Ruga to be murdered in the dark by herself.

She continued to clip the roses, nervous energy making her hands shake. At least she wasn't thinking about Elketh anymore, she thought dryly.

Ruga thought, at first, that she was imagining the footsteps. They were very soft against the flagstones that led to the garden, a muffled but rapid noise that could've been the thumping of a small animal. But then the gate scraped open.

Ruga straightened herself and turned.

CHAPTER TWENTY-NINE

A burst of energy pushed Elketh to the limits of her arm strength. She clipped the sea with her stolen oars at a steady pace, how she'd seen the fishmongers row, but she was no sailing expert. Lights smattered Vakker's harbor in the distance. She was getting somewhere.

Her biceps burned; her forearms twinged. The wood splintered at the palms of her hands, unused to the exertion of rowing. Elketh let out a scream. Another wave of energy came over her, and she swatted at the sea like she could beat it with her bare fists, the thing keeping her away from Ruga—the only thing other than herself.

She didn't know if she would make it. She didn't even know if Ruga was willing to give her another chance. But she would never forgive herself if she didn't try.

Trembling with effort, Elketh pushed and pushed herself until the speed at which each trembling oar dipped into the water had significantly decreased, until the oars were so heavy in her arms that she couldn't lift them high enough to propel the boat forward at any reliable speed. She was so, so close. The harbor loomed nearer with each passing minute.

This seemed so much more romantic in her head.

She needed a break. Elketh set the oars down and watched, with horror, as one of them slid through the oar-hole and began to float away.

She looked at the oar, riding the motion of the water in the opposite direction. She looked at the harbor, so very, very close. And she looked down at herself, at the sleek silk dress embroidered with gold thread that Isolde had helped her into earlier that day.

"Fuck it," Elketh said.

She reached her knife behind her back and cut the dress off.

In just her shift, Elketh stood, the sides of the boat rocking a bit with the new distribution of weight. She steadied herself, taking a deep breath.

And then, not for the first time, Elketh leaped into the harbor.

CHAPTER THIRTY

An apparition materialized in the gate to Ruga's garden. No, not an apparition: a bedraggled, bare-footed, pointed-eared woman in a drenched white shift that clung to her brown skin, stringy hair damp with saltwater.

"Elketh," Ruga said instinctively before her brain caught up to the image in front of her.

Elketh stumbled forward. Her teeth chattered. Ruga was too stunned to say anything else, her mouth agape in awe.

"D-did you know," said Elketh, "that there are fishwives at your harbor"—her teeth chattered violently then, and she had to ride it out before she could continue—"who are all married to each other? They were very c-concerned about an elf d-d-dragging herself to sh-shore. All f-five of them."

"You must be freezing," was the only thing Ruga could think to say. Her eyes fell to the blanket, folded up nearby. She gave it a shake to unfold it and then approached Elketh to swathe her in it.

"The water was colder than it looked," Elketh said as Ruga bundled her up.

Ruga let her hands linger on Elketh through the blanket. She took in Elketh's clumped eyelashes, her reddened eyes, her faintly blue lips. And she finally registered what had happened.

"Elketh, did you *swim* here all the way from Branwen?"

"Not the entire way," Elketh said, defensively.

Elketh—someone who went to great extremes to get what she wanted—had partially swum her way to Torden and gone straight to Ruga's rose garden without so much as drying off first. There was only one conclusion Ruga could draw from that: Elketh wanted Ruga.

Badly enough to risk her life, even.

The force of the revelation made Ruga stagger back, but Elketh stepped forward, keeping Ruga's arms encircling her.

"I spend a lot of time apologizing," Elketh started, perhaps untruthfully, "and I probably will, forever."

Ruga tried to respond, but her throat was closed with shock.

"I'm a coward," Elketh continued. "I don't like change. I'm scared of new things. I get into my habits, and I don't like to break them. But I... But you—" Her entire body shuddered under the blanket. Ruga squeezed her closer. "You make me want to change," Elketh finished pitifully.

"Elketh, you don't have to... I'm fine," Ruga insisted. "I don't need some big proclamation." Elketh had really crossed the sea for Ruga. That fact rang in Ruga's head like a joyous bell: *Elketh wants me, Elketh wants me, Elketh wants me.*

"I do have to," Elketh said. "I want the chance to ride horseback with you to the forests of Sydlig, and I want to be the one to dance first at the midsummer festival, and I want to learn to make chainmail, too. I want to beat out soldiers in drinking contests and then vomit my guts out the next morning." She batted away tears. "I want to be with you. It was dumb to leave. I couldn't get you out of my head the whole time I was gone. I shouldn't...shouldn't have done that." Weakly, she coughed into the blanket. "I'm... Will you...? Do you think that you...?"

Ruga lifted her hands to either side of Elketh's face and held her still. "Kiss me?"

Elketh's lips were cold, and she tasted of salt; her cheeks were wet with tears, and her hair wet with the ocean. It was the best kiss Ruga ever had—maybe the best kiss anybody'd ever had.

At the end of it, Elketh rested her head against Ruga's shoulder, and Ruga held her close. "To answer your question," said Ruga, "yes. I will have you back. Gladly." Ruga kissed the side of Elketh's hair, right against a ruined plait.

Elketh sniffled. "Why do you like me? I've been awful to you."

And Ruga could only laugh at that. If only Elketh knew that her stubbornness, her passion, was exactly the reason Ruga liked her. "Actually," Ruga murmured into Elketh's ear, "I love you."

Shifting so she could look Ruga in the eye, Elketh said, "I was going to say that first."

"Well, you didn't."

"You're infuriating," said Elketh.

"You *love* me," said Ruga.

"I do love you," conceded Elketh.

"You never actually said you were sorry," Ruga pointed out.

"Did I really not?"

"No."

"I usually...prepare speeches. In my head. Before I blurt my feelings all out like that. I was in a rush to get here."

That Elketh had needed to get to Ruga so urgently only made Ruga love her more.

Ruga went to kiss Elketh again. It was a sweet, drawn-out kiss, the kind shared between people who expected to have many more kisses in their future. Ruga changed her mind, then. *This* was the best kiss she'd ever had.

The next time they kissed, too, Ruga thought that one was superior. Whenever she thought back on this moment, Ruga would remember how silly it was to rank them like this—every kiss she shared with Elketh was the new best kiss of all time.

"What does this mean for Branwen?" Ruga asked when they pulled away from each other a third time. "Do you think your father would make you the heir again?"

"I don't know," Elketh said. "I wasn't really thinking about that. I can't believe you were going to marry my brother."

Ruga kissed her forehead. "We should probably send someone to let him know you didn't drown."

"I am sure my maid raised an alarm," Elketh said.

"I'll stop at the courier. You could probably use a warm bath. Let's get you inside."

"Will you draw me a bath?"

Ruga rolled her eyes. "What, you still can't draw your own bath?"

"I rowed here, and then I swam the rest of it. I can barely lift my arms," Elketh protested. For once, she had a valid excuse.

"You're drawing the next one," Ruga said, and her heart leapt because there would be a next one. There would be a next everything.

"Fine," Elketh said. They both knew if Elketh protested even a little, Ruga would do it, anyway. Ruga would do anything for her. And she didn't really mind drawing baths, after all. But Ruga suspected that Elketh would follow through because she had proven she was willing to.

Still in the blanket, Elketh began to hobble toward the gate. Ruga laughed at her, a culmination of all the joy she felt and everything she had to look forward to. Elketh turned back with a grin. "I love your laugh," she said.

"I know you do," said Ruga.

ELKETH & RUGA

Elketh and Ruga spent the next few weeks transporting Ruga's things over to Branwen and saying goodbye to their favorite places and people in Torden. They moved to new apartments within the castle more suitable for two people. Everyone suspected that the alliance between Torden and Branwen would hold off any attempts by the haughty Lynby warlords to try anything. Word had traveled that the alliance was happening sooner than expected.

The elvish king was surprisingly helpful in assisting Elketh with her agenda to make the castle as Ruga-friendly as she could. He showed her a spot on the top floor perfect for Ruga's favorite loom, with a beautiful view of the forest outside, and selected a two-story, long-abandoned ballroom, where they ordered shelves to be built so that Ruga could have a library. Elketh suspected—rightfully—that her father was very excited to be done with ruling. She heard, when she was out in town looking for a good place to build a forge, that her father had already begun construction on a small home by a lake for him and the queen to share.

Ruga was overwhelmed with Elketh's presents at first—it was like they were competing to do the most for each other, as Ruga used the loom to weave them a beautiful rug for their new bedchamber and filled the library with books not just for improving her knowledge and skill sets, but also for the kind of adventure stories Elketh was growing to like.

It didn't help that they were being flooded with gifts from all over. Olwen and Anwen sent them jewelry and swords, beautifully crafted arrows, and several live goats. Torden and Sydlig's own craftspeople stepped in—Dag the seamstress sent them, unbidden, two gorgeous dresses that happened to be perfect for a wedding ceremony, and the blacksmith who allowed Ruga to work in her forge sent them matching armbands to commemorate their union. One day, Queen Gwenhwyfar came back from a trip at sea carrying an ugly, overly ornamented crown that Elketh hoped she never had to see again, so different from Elketh's favorite neckband made by the same jeweler and blacksmith duo. It was an interesting mottle of metals, made from the old crown's remnants and the new, a symbolic linking of past to present.

Between the alliance going through and the compromise of the ceremonial crown, the tensions between Queen Astrid and King Gareth had smoothed over.

Ruga tried on the crown with tears in her eyes. Even Elketh could admit Ruga looked beautiful wearing it.

Their rooms overflowed with books and decorations; it looked very lived-in, Elketh thought, and Ruga was inclined to agree.

The best gift came one night, after several weeks of work, when Elketh suggested they take a walk around the castle. It wasn't the most hospitable place for a walk, though Ruga and Elketh had discussed improving the landscaping. They stepped over dead branches and dirt, noting the things they would like to change to each other until Elketh brought Ruga to an intricate wrought-iron gate.

"Was this here before?" Ruga asked, startled. It stood out from the rest of the castle's exterior. The dirt around it had been freshly tilled.

Elketh lifted a key from her skirts and passed it to Ruga.

"Elketh, you didn't," Ruga said.

"Don't get too excited," Elketh said. "It needs some work."

The key turned in the lock, and the gates swung open on the beginnings of a rose garden.

The garden was similar in its setup to Ruga's own at home, though there weren't nearly as many flowers. White roses entwined with wooden structures, extending upward. The area was enclosed, set against the castle wall. The familiar smell of her beloved roses nearly brought Ruga to tears.

"Some of them are transplanted from your garden," Elketh said. "I didn't want to ruin your old one in Torden, but Queen Astrid's maid seemed to think it was a good idea."

Another thing Ruga would have to thank Freya for.

"I don't really know how roses work, or when to plant them, or anything like that," Elketh continued. "But we have a trader who comes through every once in a while with flower seeds, and I have several contacts who will be on the lookout for him." Elketh pointed upward. "East-facing, like you said they should be."

Their rooms faced west—Ruga could concede with Elketh on that, and it seemed like a good idea to not have Elketh in a bad mood every morning because of the sunrise—but as Ruga followed the direction of Elketh's finger upward, she caught sight of the window to her weaving room. She would be able to look down on the garden whenever she wanted.

"I can't plant them until spring. But this is more than I could ever have hoped for." Ruga reached for Elketh's hand. "*You're* more than I could ever have hoped for."

"You're too much," Elketh objected, but Ruga could tell she liked the compliment.

"I thought I was supposed to be the one spoiling you?" Ruga teased.

"You do spoil me," Elketh said. "I'm very spoiled."

Ruga brought Elketh's fingers to her lips, smiling as she kissed them. She planned on spoiling Elketh for the rest of their lives.

Meanwhile, Branwen's steward worked nonstop, a sheen of sweat on her brow at all times, to prepare the castle for a wedding the likes of which the Elven Islands had never seen. Thinking of the grand feasts of the orcs' midsummer festival, Elketh demanded that they invite everyone in town who could come along with the dignitaries from other countries. They hired chefs and cleaning crews, performers and skalds, and brought in games and drinking horns for the festivities. To King Gareth's dismay, Elketh had the boring paintings of him taken down and replaced with lively tapestries depicting the kinds of things she'd seen over the channel.

When the fateful day finally came, Isolde helped dress both Elketh and Ruga. Elketh switched out the neckband she wore daily for a silver one that matched the gifted armband. Dag's dresses were slender, samite under lace studded with gems, and Elketh commented more than once, to Ruga's delight, about her appreciation of Ruga's figure as Isolde good-humoredly rolled her eyes.

They married on the beach to the backdrop of the sea, their bare feet digging into sand, surrounded by friends and strangers alike, there to bask in love or witness the alliance, or just for the grand meal scheduled after. King Gareth was there, as were Queen

Gwenhwyfar, Prince Owain, Queen Astrid, Freya, dignitaries from Torden and the Elven Islands, including the now-married Rhiannon and Fiona, and—Elketh could have sworn that she saw her shed a tear—Vera.

Everyone would comment, as the priestess spoke them through their vows, how it seemed that Elketh and Ruga only had eyes for each other and how deeply in love they were. Ruga caught Freya's gaze in the crowd and nodded acknowledgment to her, and then she caught her sister's, unusually teary. How lucky she was, she thought, to be so loved.

She turned back to Elketh just as the priestess finished her speech. Elketh stepped forward to stroke one of Ruga's horns as though she couldn't help herself. Ruga just looked at her—she would always look at her, because Elketh liked being looked at, and Ruga strove to give Elketh whatever she wanted—

And Elketh looked back.

THANK YOU

Thank you for taking the time to read *The Orc and Her Bride,* the first in a series of sapphic fantasy romances. If you have the time, please consider leaving an honest review on your favorite platform(s).

If you'd like to receive updates about future releases, deals, and freebies, you can sign up for my newsletter at lilagwynn.com/newsletter.

NEXT IN SERIES...

THE ORC —AND— HER SPY

In which Freya goes to extremes to protect her queen and Astrid holds her heart close against a long future ahead without her trusted spymaster.

ACKNOWLEDGEMENTS

Many people were involved in the making of this book. First and foremost, I'd like to thank Sarah Waites, without whom this book would not exist—her beautiful cover art literally inspired this story, from its tone to its gentle orc protagonist. Sarah also drew the stunning map of Torden from a very terrible sketch, which is no small feat. This book wouldn't be half as good without my beta readers, especially Ceril N. Domace, to whom any world-building that seems fleshed out can be attributed due to her astute eye and thoughtful questions; Victoria, who gave lovely, concise feedback about my weakest spots and helped strengthen my opening paragraphs; Natalia, who claimed she wanted to be Ruga when she grows up (in spite of already being grown up); and Jordan, who pushed for details and requested two to three more sex scenes (sorry). A huge thank you to my editor, Charlie Knight, for catching my numerous errant commas—any remaining grammatical errors or awkward sentences are my own. I owe my dear friends Fel and Matt for listening to my insecurities and cheering me on and my sister for diligently reading everything I write. Without the writing Discord servers I'm in, I wouldn't have the knowledge I needed to publish books or the comfort of being part of a community, and that's also true for authors Nat Paga, Mel E. Lemon, and Coyote JM Edwards, who hype me up on social media even though I've become terrible at using it. Last but not least, an enormous thank you to reviewers, especially those on my ARC list, who are joining me in this genre switch. Hopefully it wasn't too jarring.

ABOUT THE AUTHOR

Lila Gwynn is a lesbian author (and avid reader) of sapphic fantasy fiction. In her free time, she can be found binge-reading indie books, casually playing video games, or occasionally writing. She lives with her wonderful butch girlfriend and their many cats.

Bluesky: @lilagwynn.bsky.social
Instagram: @lilagwynn
Website: https://lilagwynn.com
Patreon: Patreon.com/LilaGwynn